SORRY, WRONG FAMILY

One day a mysterious package is delivered to Mrs. Bartolotti. Usually she likes surprises, but this one beats them all. Inside the package is Konrad, a seven-year-old boy who's been produced and educated in a factory and guaranteed to please in every way. Konrad does prove to be the ideal son: brilliant in school, helpful around the house, always honest and polite. It's no wonder his schoolmates hate him.

Then the factory, realizing its mistake, demands Konrad's return. Well Konrad may be *too* perfect, but to his new mom he's nonreturnable. Leave it to Mrs. Bartolotti to devise a foolproof plan that will turn Konrad into a kid the factory won't ever want back—but everyone else will!

"It's great fun."

BULLETIN OF THE CENTER FOR CHILDREN'S BOOKS

AVON CAMELOT

PUBLISHED BY AVON BOOKS

007-010

0

620

71001 00195

ISBN 0-380-62018-

P9-AWX-582

STRAWBERRY YELLOW

NAOMI HIRAHARA

PROSPECT
·PARK·
BOOKS

Published by Prospect Park Books
969 S. Raymond Avenue
Pasadena, California 91105
prospectparkbooks.com

Distributed by Consortium Book Sales & Distribution
cbsd.com

Library of Congress Cataloging-in-Publication Data
on file with Library of Congress

For reference only:
Hirahara, Naomi
Strawberry yellow / Naomi Hirahara.
ISBN 978-1-938849-02-2
1. Novelists—Fiction.   2. Mysteries—Fiction.   3. Japanese-American—Fiction.   4. California—Fiction.   I. Title.

10 9 8 7 6 5 4 3 2 1

Designed by Amy Inouye, Future Studio
Printed in the United States of America

prospectparkbooks.com

DEDICATED TO THE REAL WATSONVILLE

Author's note: Watsonville is a real place with real farms and real homes. Mas Arai's Watsonville, on the other hand, exists in a parallel universe, where the truth ends and the imagination begins. I hope that you enjoy your visit to Mas's Watsonville in these pages, but if you have an opportunity, go to the real one. It's a wonderful place.

We're trapped like rats in a wired cage,
To fret and fume with impotent rage

—**ANONYMOUS,**
*excerpt of a poem written in the
Poston War Relocation Center*

CHAPTER ONE

Shug Arai didn't have any shoulders, or at least it looked like he didn't have any. So when Mas Arai peered into the satin-lined casket to gaze at the body of his second cousin, one of the few relatives that he had in the United States, he was startled to see that someone—most likely the country mortician—had completely stuffed the top of Shug's suit jacket à la Jack LaLanne. "*Mah—okashii*," Mas's late wife, Chizuko, would have exclaimed under her breath if she were there at the viewing at the Watsonville mortuary. Funny looking. She would have been right. Even as a young man, Shug had been stooped over, bicep-free. But whatever was missing from his frame was in his brain. Shug was about the smartest man that Mas had known in both Hiroshima and California.

"I wanted the casket lined with strawberries, but the family wouldn't hear of it." A rough-hewn voice boomed behind Mas. "In fact, I thought he should be buried in his strawberry plot."

The familiar voice belonged to a familiar face. Rectangular like a television set, piercing eyes and thick lips. Deep lines were on the forehead and the hair had thinned out and become the texture and color of fishing line. But Mas still could make the ID. "Oily?" he asked.

"Fifty years later, and I still can pick you out from across the room. Glad you were able to make it." Oily grabbed Mas's head and hugged it to his chest like a pigskin football. Mas normally wouldn't have tolerated such behavior, but he was back in his birthplace and the town where he spent his early adult years. He'd allow Oily one hug for old time's sake. But only one.

"Everyone will be here tomorrow. Everyone. Be a mini-reunion of our time in the Stem House. How long did you live in the house, anyway?"

"Three year. But not straight through. I'zu go ova to Texas, pickin' tomatoes. And San Francisco, schoolboy, before they kick me out."

"Then you made your way to L.A. You diversified, just like Shug. The rest of us homebodies, we just stayed here."

Mas couldn't put himself in the same category as Shug. Mas was a no-good gardener in L.A., while Shug was a famous breeder, the father of new strawberry varieties, informally referred to as Dr. Ichigo, or Dr. Strawberry. Shug was wanted in places, like France and Chile, just for his horticultural expertise. After he circled the world a few times, he had plopped back here in Watsonville, California.

"I was surprised, too, that he decided to retire here. But he told me he had some unfinished business in Watsonville."

Mas scratched the back of his right ear. *Unfinished business.*

Oily nodded. "Who knows what that meant? Maybe he knew that strawberry yellows was going to hit Watsonville again."

"*Ya-ro?*"

"Yeah, yellows. A disease as mean as you can get. Stunts the growth of the fruit, for one thing, and also the leaves start curling up, get spotty and yellow. Worst yet, it spreads all over the place   not only to the second generation, but back even to the mothers. Nasty business. Practically wiped out strawberries in California in the twenties. And now it's taken up here again."

Oily was obviously still involved with strawberries, but Mas had heard that he was no longer with Sugarberry, one of the town's oldest cooperatives.

"You'zu not wiz Sugarberry no more?"

Oily shook his head. "Everbears, the new kid in town. You know what these young people are into these days. Organic. But also high-tech. It's run by a guy who made his millions on the Internet. He's from around here, Monterey. Wanted to retire as a gentlemen farmer, or should I say boy farmer. He's only thirty."

Mas raised his eyebrows. Thirty didn't make this CEO a boy, but a baby.

"Hey, this company has potential. Really. Even Billy has come on board."

Billy was Shug's only son. There had been some talk— Mas couldn't remember how he heard—that the two hadn't been getting along, especially when Billy had taken a job with a new strawberry . . . outfit, the outfit apparently being Everbears.

"Billy's doing good. Coming up with a new variety to fight strawberry yellow. Daddy was doing the same, too, or so I heard."

"Shug's no-finish bizness?"

"Don't know if that's what he was referring to, but he wasn't able to finish it, for near that I could tell . . ." Both

Oily and Mas glanced back at the casket. Next to it on an easel was a blown-up photo of Shug, probably taken in the 1990s, mounted on foam core. Typeset on the bottom of the image: **Shigeo "Shug" Arai, 1929–2004.**

Oily turned back toward Mas. "Anyway, the whole gang, well at least the ones who are still alive, can't wait to see you. Remember Evelyn? She had a mean crush on you back then. Some of us joked that she was the reason you ran away to Los Angeles."

Mas bit down on the right side of his dentures so hard that the left side almost became dislodged.

"Yep, she was excited to hear about you coming. She lost Hank a couple of years ago. You haven't remarried, have you?"

Mas shook his head, his ears burning while he thought of Genessee Howard. Mas's best friend Haruo referred to Genessee as Mas's lady friend, but it hadn't even gone that far— no, not with his three-year-old grandson Takeo bursting into rooms at the most inopportune times.

"Howsu Minnie?" Mas changed the subject and asked about Shug's widow.

"You can ask her yourself. Family will be coming in a few minutes," Oily reported.

"Oh, I gotsu go." Mas tapped his Casio watch. He'd made it a point to attend the visitation an hour earlier just to avoid contact with old relatives and friends. "Gotsu some things to do," he lied.

Oily looked disappointed. "Well, we'll all see you tomorrow at the Buddhist church. Food in the gym afterwards. You won't leave without seeing everyone, right?"

Mas nodded. He took care not to slip on dead leaves on

the mortuary's walkway as he returned to the Ford truck. He was staying at a nearby discount motel. Haruo, who continued to see a counselor in Little Tokyo for his gambling addiction, often spoke of something called "space." Although Mas thought counseling was purely hocus pocus, he sure found that he needed some space these days. And this solo visit to Watsonville, even though it was under very sad circumstances, had come at the perfect time.

When he went to his room, there was no crying, no arguing, in fact no sounds at all, aside from the hum of the mildewed wall air conditioner. Dozing off on the flimsy mattress was pure heaven; that is, until he heard a rapping on the door.

Mas shook his head out of its wooziness and approached the door. "Whozu dat?"

"Billy. Shug's son."

Mas pulled back the drapes and sure enough, there was the tall, thin frame of Billy Arai. He was in the plus side of middle age, and Mas could clearly see that he was taking his old man's posture. Mas sensed through the cheap glass window that Billy wasn't in his right mind tonight. But out of respect for the dead Shug, he opened the motel door.

Billy's clothing had the sour tang of beer. He was wearing a red polo shirt with "Everbears Strawberries" stitched over his heart. The last time Mas had seen Billy, he'd been a college student, with long, shaggy hair that the young people had at the time. Billy's hair was now cropped short, at least in the back.

"Oily told me you were staying here," Billy said. "I'm going over to the house, and I thought you might want to come."

"Now?" It was edging toward midnight. "Anyway, thought the house all close up."

"But not the greenhouses. The greenhouses are still ours."

Mas felt a pang of nostalgia. Although the Stem House was only a few blocks away from the motel, he had avoided passing by. He couldn't stand seeing it uninhabited, abandoned. The house deserved a truckload of people and children running through its rooms. To see it boarded up, essentially dead, would be painful, yet Mas was curious. He wouldn't have gone on his own accord, but now, being pushed by Billy, he found himself motivated. He grabbed the keys to his old truck and followed Billy to the motel parking lot. The full moon was bright white, like a policeman's interrogation lamp.

"I drive," Mas insisted. He wasn't about to have Billy get behind the wheel.

"Okay," Billy relented. "Just wait a minute." He went over to a large pickup truck, a new model, and pulled out a six-pack of beer from the passenger's side.

Shug's son wasn't taking his father's death well. Not at all. It had been a heart attack, that's what Oily had told Mas a week ago over the phone. Minnie had been away down south in Santa Maria to babysit their grandchildren, and Billy was the one who was supposed to check in on his father. Mas heard that Shug died alone.

Billy didn't have to tell Mas how to get to the Stem House. It was second nature to travel on the familiar dirt road. There was a cluster of small houses, farmworkers' temporary housing, and then looming, like a dark giant creature curled up and taking a rest in the fields, was the Stem House.

Mas pulled into the dirt driveway and parked next to a couple of glass greenhouses.

Mas still didn't know how the Stem House was lost. Nobody really talked about it, and Mas, being a second cousin, didn't feel it was his business to ask.

Billy offered Mas a beer but he shook his head. At least one of them had to be sober-minded. Mas resented that it had to be him instead of Billy.

The silhouette of the Stem House was the same, but the details were all wrong. The wood siding was decayed and falling off, like the scales of a sick fish. The windows were nailed shut like the closed eyes of a corpse; the boarded-up door was the silenced mouth. All its grand furnishings had long since been fleeced, probably sold at pawn shops.

Mas felt almost like crying, not just about the house, but about the past and the memory of those who had once brought so much life to its rooms. Was this their fate, too? To rot, to be forgotten or avoided?

Billy averted his eyes from the house, as if it pained him to see it in such condition. He took out a small flashlight connected to his keychain and aimed it toward a patch of dirt next to the greenhouse.

In contrast to the dilapidated house, the plot was full of new growth. Mas saw five rows of strawberry plants, all carefully labeled with something white and thin stuck in the ground.

Billy bent down and Mas did the same.

"These are my father's test plants." The flashlight revealed small red strawberries about the size of a quarter. "And you see what he calls these—"

Mas took out the white plastic knife that was stuck in the ground and read the writing in Shug's careful script. "Masao," he said out loud, amazed. "Datsu my name."

Billy nodded. "He named this variety after you. This is his special one, the one that was supposed to take the industry by storm. He told Oily once that he owed you one." Billy then fell silent, as if he wanted to hear the reason why. But Mas could not offer one.

"Yah, well, your daddy and me got along."

"Must have been more than get along. My dad always said you two were thick as thieves."

Mas remembered when he first met Shug outside the same greenhouse. He was dropped off by a family friend who had picked him up from the port in San Francisco.

"Arai." Mas introduced himself, awkwardly sticking out his hand. He was told by his family in Hiroshima that's what the Americans did. Mas had been born in Watsonville, but he had spent most of his young life in Japan.

Shug ignored Mas's extended hand. He was wearing plastic-rimmed glasses and his hair was slicked back with oil. "I know that's your name," he replied. "Most of us are Arais here. But what's your first name? You know, first name."

Mas struggled to follow his second cousin's English. He had only gone up to junior high and languages, especially foreign ones, were never his strong suit. "Masao."

"We had a number of Masaos at Watsonville High School. You can be Mas."

Mas frowned. Mas? What kind of shit name was that? Just a few hours back in California, and these Americans were already trying to change his identity. "Masao," he declared loudly. "My name izu Masao."

"C'mon, Mas, come to the house." Shug lifted Mas's wicker suitcase onto his sunken shoulder.

Mas scowled but followed. What could he do? He'd made the decision to make a life for himself in America and he had to play by their rules, at least until he could afford his own place. He would *gaman*, grit his teeth, and put up with this new living arrangement and new roommates for now.

Anyway, he was worn out. Two weeks stuffed in the cheapest section of a boat had been suffocating. As a result, he was in an especially foul mood. So foul that he almost missed out on the impact of what stood right in front of him in the middle of strawberry fields. A Victorian two-story house of pure white, complete with a porch, round tower, and steep roof.

"Looks nice, huh? We just got it painted after we got it back from Arizona."

"House yours?"

"Well, now it is. Had to go to court to get it back. But yes, it's ours. Architect named Stem, so everyone around here calls it the Stem House."

Mas had never seen a house so grand. It could have been Truman's White House for all he knew.

"I have to warn you," said Shug, stepping up to the porch. "We have a lot of folks living here. Actually, we had even more before."

"Family?"

"Some are. Some aren't. Ever since we got the house back, it's been Grand Central Station. Mostly Poston, especially from Camp Two like us. A few from Heart Mountain and Minidoka. Even some Tule Lakers. There used to be even more."

Mas, at the time, had no idea what Shug was talking about.

A large teenager clutching a football stood in the doorway.

"This is Ouya Takei. But we call him Oily."

"Hey, Hiroshima boy's here. We've been waiting for you. Want to hear all your stories of how you survived the A-bomb."

"Don't listen to him. He's *baka*." Shug pushed Oily aside.

Mas was surprised to hear the Japanese insult come out of his second cousin's mouth.

"Hey, I know what *baka* means." Oily called out as they walked through the living room to the staircase.

Standing in the second-floor hallway were three girls. Teenage girls with strange curly hair teased and tied in kerchiefs and scarves. One of them, Minnie, wore plastic-framed glasses the shape of cat's eyes.

"Here he is. Mas. Before you all drool over him, let him relax, okay? He's been on a boat for two weeks and needs to get his land legs back."

"Hi, Mas."

"Hello, Mas."

"Good to meet you, Mas."

The three called out to him as Oily entered one of the corner rooms.

"This will be your bedroom. You'll be bunking with me and Oily."

Across from a bunk bed was an unmade twin bed, sheets and blankets still tangled together. On the floor below a bay window sat a mattress, which is where Shug dropped the wicker suitcase.

Through the walls, Mas heard the laughter of girls.

"So what do you think?" Shug asked. "You think you'll be all right here?"

Out the window was a view of two greenhouses and beyond that, straight rows of strawberry plants. Mas finally smiled. "I like."

Billy had stepped away from the test plot, so Mas couldn't help but sneak in a taste of the Masao. He pulled off one of the larger berries. It was firm, a meaty chew with a sweetness that tasted familiar. He remembered the berries developed early by the University of California, the Shasta and Lassen. This one wasn't that different from the Shasta, he thought. What was so special about the Masao?

Ban! Ban! The clattering of wood hitting wood.

Shug's son was on the porch of the Stem House, pulling off the slats over the door with his bare hands.

Mas frowned. Had the boy gone *kuru-kuru-pa*? He moved as quickly as possible in the darkness. The decaying stairs creaked under his weight, the top one almost collapsing.

"Whatchu doin'?" Mas hissed, even though there was no one around. "Not your house no more."

Billy tugged at an especially stubborn three-by-five. "Don't worry. Nobody cares."

Mas picked up the flashlight from the porch so he could get a better look at what Billy was trying to do.

"Youzu bleedin'."

Billy didn't stop. "You gonna help me then?" he said, as the door frame seemed to moan in pain.

"*Chotto, chotto.*" Mas cursed, first at Billy and then at himself. Whatthehell was the boy thinking? Why did he agree to come in the first place?

Taking the flashlight with him, Mas stumbled back to the Ford and pushed the front seat, a junkyard find, forward. He grabbed hold of a hammer, saw, and crowbar and then felt the floor for another flashlight.

He presented his finds to Billy, who had collapsed on the porch, sweat running down his face. He was gulping down another beer. "My dad was right. He said you were always prepared for anything."

Together, with the tools, they easily completed the extraction. Billy, of course, entered first. Mas, clutching his flashlight and the crowbar, followed.

The inside of the house smelled awful. A mixture of piss and mold and body odor. Billy immediately began to sneeze, and Mas attempted to breathe out of his mouth.

There was still some old furniture left in the house, some even old enough to be from Mas's day. But it was all beaten down and soiled, no use to anyone.

"They found vagrants sleeping inside the house. Almost set the house on fire. Boarded it up. Some of them have since moved into the greenhouse. There was even talk of a dead body found in here once."

Mas didn't doubt it.

The house was terribly rain damaged. Mold had grown and died in every crevice and corner.

"We needsu to get outta here," Mas said, hearing some kind of noise upstairs.

"Don't worry. It's probably just a rat."

Mas didn't understand why Billy wanted to come inside the house. It almost seemed as though he was looking for something. But what? What good could come out of this mess of a house that wasn't taken already?

Before Mas could stop him, Billy was climbing up the staircase, which obviously wasn't in the most stable condition.

"I'zu leavin'," he declared, but that didn't stop Billy. *Maybe I can call someone for help. Oily?*

But Mas had no cell phone and there was no working phone that he could see.

Shikataganai. Mas could only follow Billy up the stairs like a good-for-nothing sheep.

He saw Billy disappear into the corner room, the round room where Mas had slept when he lived there. When he walked in the door, he saw that Shug's son had collapsed on one of the beds, clutching a couple of his leftover beers.

Sonafugun. Mas shook Billy, but he obviously was out, at least for the night.

Mas shivered, hearing something moving in the corner of the room. What now? If he left the drunken man and Billy fell down the decrepit stairs by himself, Mas would be haunted for the rest of his life.

No, once he opened the motel door to Billy and had

driven them both to the Stem House, he had made a commitment to see this thing through. He chose the mattress (it couldn't have been the same mattress from the 1940s, could it?) on the floor by the window. Zipping up his windbreaker so no stray bugs or rodents could gain entry, he lay down and willed himself to sleep. Everything will be all right in the morning, he told himself. He'd go to the funeral and then get into the Ford and be on his way back home. As he drifted off, he apologized to his daughter, grandson, and even son-in-law. In spite of the all the *monku* that he'd expressed silently and not so silently about them, life with them was a picnic compared to this.

Sirens, not his grandson's cry, roused Mas from his sleep.

Sunlight came through the slats of wood hammered over the windows.

He looked at the mattress where Billy had been sleeping. It was empty.

The sirens, meanwhile, were getting louder and louder. Mas pressed his face to the slats, feeling splinters burn his cheeks. First he saw the police cars. A few minutes later, a white car with an emblem proclaiming the Santa Cruz County Sheriff-Coroner's Office pulled into the dirt driveway.

CHAPTER TWO

It had been a dog that discovered the body. A purplish-colored pit bull that was now wagging his tail by his owner's feet. He was chewing on an old discarded baseball mitt, apparently his reward for his find.

The only thing that Mas could make out from the dog's owner was that it was the body of a woman. A dead homeless vagrant, Mas figured. One of the trespassers that Billy had been talking about. Mas wanted to get out of there as soon as possible, but his Ford was completely surrounded by the police cars. Even worse, an officer had opened the truck's door and was doing a full-scale search. Mas saw him opening the glove compartment—it would only be a matter of minutes until they identified him as the owner. So he stepped forward.

"Sorry, this is a crime scene. You'll have to stand behind the tape." A policeman tried to shoo Mas away.

Mas saw a stretcher being carried toward the greenhouse.

"Dis my truck," he said.

"This is your truck? Lieutenant—we have the owner of the vehicle here."

Mas had dealt with his share of policemen and women, so he braced himself for probing questions, perhaps even skepticism.

The lieutenant was an Asian woman, her hair streaked with gray and secured back in a bun. One of her officers handed over the Ford's registration papers.

"You are Masao Arai?"

Mas nodded.

"I've heard of you."

Mas widened his eyes.

"I think we are distantly related. My name is Robin Arai."

Mas and the lieutenant played family tree for at least ten minutes. He figured out that this Robin was Shug's niece. She was Billy's cousin, and she'd pretty much been raised by Shug and Minnie. The father had died in Chicago in some freak accident in the fifties, shortly after this girl Robin had been born.

"You're here for Uncle Shug's funeral."

Mas nodded.

"I live in dis house," he explained.

"In the forties, right? After World War Two?"

He nodded again.

"So you came here last night to take a trip down memory lane."

"Nah, well, Billy—" Mas was in a quandary about how much he should share about Shug's son being the one to come here in the first place.

"Was Billy here?"

Mas now regretted spilling the beans.

"Did I hear that right? Billy Arai was here last night?" A man as short as Mas interrupted their conversation. He wore the same uniform as hers, except that his narrow nametag read, "Sergeant Arturo Salgado."

Mas felt his face grow hot. He could taste the unbrushed crud in the back of his dentures.

"It's okay, Sergeant, I have this covered."

Someone called Robin over to the greenhouse. She abruptly excused herself, leaving Mas alone with Salgado.

"I bet you have it covered," Salgado muttered to himself. "Covering your family's ass as always."

Mas was shocked to hear the insult coming from the police officer's mouth. Robin and Sergeant Salgado were supposedly on the same team, but obviously that team was divided.

"So you're an Arai, too," Salgado said. His ears looked normally shaped, but he seemed to have the gift of excellent hearing, or perhaps more like eavesdropping. "Why would you come to this place last night?"

Mas's eyes inadvertently moved toward the test strawberry plot. The rows of Masaos were missing, quite evident to his gardener's eyes. What was going on?

"Sergeant—" Robin called Salgado over to the crime scene.

"You don't leave," he ordered, gesturing at Mas with a stern index finger.

Mas shuffled his feet and then sneaked a look past the officers toward the open door of the greenhouse. He expected to see the wasted body of a homeless woman. Dirty, maybe even toothless.

But it was a young woman, maybe thirty years old at most, with a sheet of brilliant blonde hair, the roots soaked with blood.

Mas dutifully waited as the police officers traveled back and forth from their parked vehicles and the scene of the crime.

What the hell had happened to Billy, Mas wondered. His truck wasn't in the motel parking lot, so somehow he'd made it back home.

But when? And why didn't he bother to wake Mas up?

In the light of day, Mas got a clearer picture of his former home. The two greenhouses hadn't changed much since he'd lived there. A few cracked windows and a haphazard arrangement of seedlings in long wooden boxes—today it looked like pansies, tomatoes, peppers, and maybe some early lettuce. Strawberries didn't need the heat; they worked better in Watsonville's mild temperatures. That's why strawberries had become the main crop for the area.

Mas ran his hand through his thinning hair. What the hell was he going to tell the police? That he fell asleep and had no idea where Billy had gone in the middle of the night? But why in the world would Billy want to hurt a young *hakujin* woman? Even if Mas told the truth, Billy would be cleared immediately. Billy would tell them where he had gone and the police could then go on and find the real killer.

But while the officers went back and forth doing their investigation, Mas noticed Sergeant Salgado's frequent glances toward him, as if he expected Mas to attempt to escape. *I'm not guilty*, he said to himself, although for some reason, he was starting to feel that he had done something wrong.

Mas hoped it would be the Arai in the uniform who would return to his side, but it was Salgado instead.

"I have some questions for you." The sergeant removed a thin notebook from his breast pocket. "What time did you come here?"

That Mas did know. Midnight.

"Midnight? That's mighty late to be traipsing around here."

"My relative's funeral. Couldn't sleep," Mas lied. He had been sleeping like a baby until Billy had come around.

"You were with Billy last night."

Mas just grunted.

"How did he seem?"

Kuru-kuru-pa. Head turned around. Also, not to mention, stinking drunk. "Fine."

"Why did you come here to the Stem House? It's not the Arai family's any more."

"Ole times' sake." That much was true.

"So it was your idea."

Mas moistened his lips.

"Maybe," was the best he could offer.

Salgado walked over to the crumbling stairs of the Stem House, and Mas followed. The fog had burnt off a little, and the sunlight accentuated the decrepit state of the building. If the house could talk, it would be moaning in pain and moaning loud.

"We could charge you with breaking and entering," Salgado said, gesturing toward the pile of torn four-by-fours, the rusty nails bent but still in the wood.

Salgado ducked to avoid a spider's web hanging from the porch eaves and the two men looked inside the open doorway. From the foot of the stairs, Mas could see the edge of

the staircase banister, the end of it shaped like an eagle's tal-
on. How many times had he, Shug, and Oily slid down that
banister? Shug's parents never scolded them or told them
not to. Boys will be boys must have been their motto, even
though they were on the cusp of being young men. The Arais
in Watsonville had taken Mas in without requiring anything
from him. If they hadn't vouched for him, there was no way
he could have returned to his birthplace, America, so early
in his life.

"Were you with Billy the whole night?"

Ah, the million-dollar question.

"Mr. Arai, you may want to protect Billy, but he's not
protecting you. You could be an accessory to murder. If
you're innocent, I would speak up."

"Ah, Billy go home," Mas said. That he spoke the half-
truth shocked even himself. He knew, however, that once he
dove into these waters, there was no going back.

"Do you remember what time?"

"*Sugu.* Right away."

"So you saw Billy Arai leave the premises. Didn't hang
around outside."

Mas shook his head, using all his might to steady his
shaking legs and arms.

"So you are the one who drank all these beers?"

There were at least three empty beer cans littering the
hallway.

Mas nodded. Maybe being drunk could be his excuse
for telling lies to the police. Only he was quite sober at this
particular time.

"Well, we'll confirm these details with Billy," said

Salgado, scribbling Mas's motel room number in his note-book. "The Forever Inn, right? Okay, you're free to go, for now. But I wouldn't leave town if I were you."

I won't, Mas thought. At least not for the rest of the day. After going back to the motel and showering, Mas dressed in the only suit he had, his funeral suit. Arriving at the temple, he sat in his usual place, the back row. Lieu-tenant Robin Arai obviously didn't have time to change out of her uniform and was already sitting in the second row. Mas couldn't see if Billy was in the customary place of the grieving son in the front.

Wreaths were everywhere. Mostly red and white, as if they all were celebrating the winning horse in the Kentucky Derby. One covered in red roses in the front had a white sash with the name "Sugarberry" glittering in silver. Right beside it, as if it were in a competition, was a more unusual arrange-ment, almost Japanese-looking, with irises, pine branches, and bamboo leaves. That one had a large sign, "Everbears."

The lesser wreaths spilled out into the aisles. There was a sad pot of Easter lilies that was in danger of being squashed by passersby. On a stake in the pot was a three-by-five card with a logo for the University of California Agriculture Department.

The only bad thing about sitting in the back was that sometimes you ended up in the front of the incense line. When it was time, Mas was directed by a mortuary worker in white gloves to line up in the center aisle. A thin *haku-jin* man in a simple long-sleeved t-shirt stood in front of him. Mas thought that the man—or was he just a teenag-er?—might have wandered into the wrong funeral, but he obviously understood the drill.

Bow, pinch the powdered incense and sprinkle it into another larger pot, and bow again. Bow in front of the golden altar. Then bow in front of Shug's open casket and take a quick look. Finally, a bow toward the family.

As he waited for his turn, Mas tried to keep his eyes right in front of him, but they wandered to the front row where the family sat.

He saw the widow, Minnie, first. Instead of her once trademark cat glasses, she was wearing rimless ones. She was one of these women who strangely looked more youthful as she aged. Sitting next to her was Billy, who made a point of looking away when Mas passed by. His two weeping sisters, each of them with a child, managed polite smiles. In the second row, Mas recognized Billy's wife—what was her name again?—from some old photo Christmas cards. Next to the wife were Billy's children, a girl and boy, all grown up.

After pinching incense and bowing a number of times, Mas was finally face-to-face with his old friend again. Shug, of course, was in the same position, but now there were other things surrounding him—teddy bears, children's drawings, Buddhist rosaries, and a baseball bat that Mas recognized as the one Shug's father, Wataru, had carved in Poston camp.

As soon as Mas returned to his seat, his legs still shaking, he heard, "Mas. Mas Arai, is that you?" A woman with shoe-polish black hair was stuffing an apron into her purse. She slid in an empty seat on his right side.

"Evelyn," Mas said weakly.

Her face was powdered white and her lipstick was too bright of a red—for both her age and the circumstances.

After unnecessarily explaining that she had been working in the kitchen—like Mas even needed an explanation—she began whispering the latest gossip about the Arai clan.

"I heard that Billy's drunk." Evelyn's breath was warm and stank of cheap coffee. "He stumbled in here, in just a t-shirt and jeans, around ten o'clock in the morning. The minister didn't know what to do. The minister's wife gave him three cups of coffee. That's not even his suit—it's one that the church was going to donate to Goodwill."

Mas bent down and patted down his hair.

"Hope that he doesn't get back in trouble again. It was an accident, it's all behind him, but some folks always bring up the past."

Like you doing now, Mas thought, although he wasn't sure what Evelyn was talking about.

"I mean, I told everyone, what did they expect? First his father dies and now his girlfriend?"

Mas sat up. "Girlu friend?" Billy was married. And his wife was right there in the Buddhist temple.

"You mean you didn't hear? He left his wife for this *hakujin* girl, Laila Smith. They've been living together for a couple of months now. She was found dead in the Stem greenhouse this morning."

The rest of the funeral was a complete blur. Evelyn tried to coax Mas into the gym for the potluck, but Mas had to insist—no, in fact almost fight his way back to the motel. He left Evelyn and headed out to the parking lot.

"Mas, Mas."

Now what? He turned.

"You're not leaving, are you, Mas?"

Mas was surprised that the newly minted widow, Minnie, even had time to bother with him, not with the crowd who wanted her attention.

"I needsu to go back home. Mari and my grandson livin' with me now. Gotsu to help them out," he flat-out lied.

Minnie laughed. "You haven't changed. You never cared for crowds. But, please, come to my house after the luncheon. Please. I have something to discuss with you."

Minnie was the one who helped Mas learn some English, as limited as it was back then. And also a few Spanish words—she said that sometimes Spanish, more than English, was more useful in what would become Mas's working world.

"Shug told me that if I could trust anyone, it would be you."

Mas grunted and looked down at the graveled ground. Minnie knew how to effectively throw punches, and now she had aimed one right at his heart. So in this round, she was the winner. He promised to stop by in the evening after dinner, releasing the widow back to the mourners, who were busy eating marinated chicken wings in the gym.

Minnie didn't mince words when Mas came by her house later on. "I think somebody killed Shug."

"I thought it was heart attack," he said.

"They say heart attack after a bout of stomach flu, but

I don't believe it. He was as strong as a horse." Minnie explained how she'd been in Santa Barbara for a week to babysit her daughters' children. Shug hadn't shown up for his weekly Monday lunch at the local Japanese restaurant, so Oily, worried, had called Billy. "Billy was the one who found him." A cry crept up Minnie's throat. "He'd been dead for maybe nine hours."

Mas could only imagine how gruesome the discovery had been. No wonder Billy seemed so tortured.

"I ordered an autopsy, but they didn't find anything unusual. No trauma. No broken bones. But the toxicology report will take a few weeks. There will be something there, you mark my words. That's why I'm not cremating him—just in case."

She folded her hands in her lap. "There is something else, too." She got up and gestured for Mas to follow her into a smaller room off the hallway.

The white room had a large desk in the middle. Shug's study, Mas figured. Minnie slid open one of the desk drawers and pointed down. Mas had to step closer to look down at its contents. A gun—not the old hunting gun he and Shug once used to shoot old strawberry baskets for target practice. No, a new, sleek, black gun that was reserved for human targets.

"Shug never had a gun like this before."

"You'zu neva see it?"

Minnie shook her hand. "No, this is new. New, as in right before he died." She quickly closed the drawer as if hiding it would deny its existence. "And this computer—" Minnie knocked on the outside of a silver laptop with a bent index finger. "This computer is not the same one that he had

when I left. I don't know what's happened to the old one."
They returned back to the living room couch.

"Shug was semi-retired, but you can't keep a breeder
from his work," Minnie said. "He wouldn't discuss it with
me. He'd go to his test plots by the greenhouse and I don't
know where else. He was keeping whatever he was doing
hush-hush. Something is fishy, Mas, and I need you to find
out what it is."

"Oily talkin' about unfinished bizness."

"I don't know what that's all about. I mean, I know his
father and Jimi Jabami's father had been experimenting with
something way back in the twenties. Not sure if it was a new
strawberry variety or maybe a secret pesticide. Don't know if
that was what Shug was working on."

The front door then opened and a giant Everbears wreath
appeared, followed by two other displays of flowers.

"My grandson, Zac, and granddaughter, Alyssa," Minnie
introduced with pride. The two college-age young people
stepped out from behind the wreaths and took turns shaking
Mas's hand. The boy was thin, tall, and too hunched over for
his age, while the girl had dark circles underneath her eyes,
but otherwise looked surprisingly fresh-faced after hours of
being bathed in incense.

"And you remember Billy."

Appearing from behind a wilting bouquet of roses was
Billy, who barely nodded an acknowledgment. Mas recipro-
cated with a half-nod of his own. Was this the killer of the
woman with the yellow hair? Or was it the crushed figure of
a man who had experienced a double dose of death on the
same day?

"Sorry," Mas said, at a loss for what more he could say. Even "sorry," perhaps, was too much. It could mean sorry for his dead father, sorry for the dead girlfriend, or maybe even sorry for the expedition to the Stem House. Or maybe all three.

Billy barely grunted.

"It's been a hard day for all of us," Minnie offered as a weak apology for her son's apparent rudeness. "And especially for Billy."

"You never liked her." Billy's heavy eyebrows hooded his eyes in the dimly lit room.

"That doesn't mean I'm not sad, horrified." She turned to Mas, her face twisted in embarrassment. "Billy had something tragic happen to his friend last night."

"She wasn't just my friend, Mom. She was my fiancée."

"You can't be married and have a fiancée."

"Dad's gone, Mom. Let's be real for once, okay?"

"I gotsu go." Mas had had enough. He'd peered down into the depths of Shug's domestic life and didn't wish to go any further, at least for today.

Before he left the house, Minnie squeezed his callused hand hard. "We'll talk more later this week. You can stay a few more days, *ne*?"

Ah, *tsukamaita*, mourned Mas. He was caught like an undersize trout lured by fluorescent pink Power Bait. This hook could not be easily extracted, so admitting defeat, he nodded yes. He was on the radar of the Watsonville Police Department anyway, so he might not have any choice in the matter.

He'd barely taken two steps outside from the front door when he felt someone pulling him back on the porch. Not surprisingly, it was Billy. Mas didn't know how to react. Was this the face of a killer?

"I heard what you said to Sergeant Salgado," he said. "Thank you."

News traveled fast, and Mas had no doubt that it had been Robin who was the news spreader.

"Where'su you last night?" Billy at least owed him an explanation.

"I woke up in the middle of night. Had a nightmare and had to get out of there. I just walked to the motel and drove myself back home. Didn't want to bother you by waking you up."

No, instead you decided to leave an old man alone in a haunted house. *Domo arigato*, thought Mas.

"I didn't kill her. I have no idea what she was doing in that greenhouse. I just blame myself for not being with her last night. If I was, she'd probably—" Billy turned away to hide his face.

"She gotsu enemies?"

Billy swallowed. "Well, there are people out there that don't like her. But to kill her? No, nobody would go that far."

"Police gonna ask you some questions. I cover for you, you knowsu."

"I'm going in tomorrow morning. Just want to thank you for trusting me. Sergeant Salgado would just love to pin this on me. Your story will make it harder for him to do that."

They heard Minnie's voice calling for Billy. "I have to go back in. I'll talk to you more later." Billy squeezed Mas's elbow, which only confirmed that they were co-conspirators. As he proceeded down the porch stairs, Mas felt his body being shaken with the pounding bass of the sound system next door. An old Impala sedan with a black hardtop pulled up to the curb. Mas couldn't help but stare at the car. *Natsukashii*. It was indeed nostalgic because he had the same model Impala at one time. In the heat of Southern California, his daughter Mari used to complain that her bare legs would sizzle on the vinyl seats when he drove her home from summer swimming lessons.

A teenager in a gray hooded sweatshirt got out of the driver's seat. "Whaddaya lookin' at?" he challenged Mas.

Mas just shrugged his shoulders and looked down as he made his way to his truck. Nostalgia was a dangerous thing and so far, coming back to Watsonville had led to nothing but trouble.

CHAPTER THREE

The fog had cleared some, but not completely. Long, opaque fingers stubbornly held onto the edges of the chocolate-brown furrows. Mas knew that strawberry picking started early, but not as early as he'd imagined. He parked the Ford along a dirt road on Jimi Jabami's farm. It was a relatively small one, only about five acres, just a postage stamp compared to the immense farms that paid allegiance to the kingdoms of larger distributors. Jimi was definitely on the side of Sugarberry, a smaller cooperative that was founded by his father and four other Japanese partners, including Shug's father.

A few minutes before seven, the cars started arriving. Minivans, Toyota sedans, old Buicks—all in better shape than Mas's truck. The pickers, both men and women, seemed in better shape than Mas as well. They were mostly in their twenties and late thirties, wearing hoodie sweatshirts and tying bandanas over their mouths. He was surprised to see some kind of manager in the fields; the old Jimi that he'd known was more hands-on. The manager checked all the pickers in; there was obviously some kind of routine. Mas had heard that everything was regulated now, with the government wanting a piece of every transaction.

The strawberry boxes were more streamlined, but other than that, not much had changed in the actual picking. For harvesting most fruits and vegetables, machines had taken over, because hadn't they taken over much of everything? But strawberries were different. Their red meat was delicate, easily bruised. The only way to pick them off their stems was with human hands. Hands that belonged to a body that was constantly hunched over.

Someone turned on an old battery-powered radio and Spanish-language music spilled out over the furrows. Mas preferred to do his outside work in silence. Nothing was completely silent, of course, when you were working with gasoline-powered blowers or even equipment that was unplugged or unmotorized. There was the *gari-gari* of the rake and the *shu-shu* of the water from the hose. Work was music to him, so he didn't think much of these pickers' selection. But then, the manager probably figured that if the beat leads to one extra box of strawberries being packed, then let the beat go on.

The pickers ignored Mas because he seemed like just part of the landscape. Another old Japanese farmer whose days were numbered. A new generation had arrived, and they, like the old, were here to stay.

Jimi Jabami wasn't a gossip or the town's historian, but he was a watcher. He watched people fight. He watched people say *warukuchi* about someone else when his or her back was turned. He watched couples exchange knowing glances before sneaking into packing sheds and corporate offices after hours.

He was as predictable and ever-present as a daily vitamin or blood pressure medicine. Seemingly innocuous, but if you ignored him, you might be risking your life.

Jimi watched a familiar figure from his kitchen window. The body was certainly that of an Arai, short and sinewy. The face had that kind of openness that could be welcoming if bent with a smile. But it was turned inward, the mouth a straight line. The man was watching the fields and now the house.

Jimi had seen this Arai at the funeral. This one sat in the back, and that was the first sign that he might be trouble. Jimi could deal with men who had to be at the front of the line, the center of attention. Hadn't Shug, in fact, been that kind of man? Jimi hoped that Shug had suffered like he and his family had suffered, would suffer, but his death seemed almost not eventful enough. Jimi looked out the window. This Arai was now walking up the walkway to his door. He would let him in.

To Mas, Jimi Jabami actually looked about the same as back in the 1940s, but only because he'd resembled an old man for most of his life. His face was broad and his eyes bulged out slightly like an owl's. And now, with the crown on Jimi's head pure white, Mas, more than ever, could imagine a supernatural version of the old man perched on a tree. Jimi was known as being one of the best cooks in town, celebrated for his pies and cakes. He had apparently been a junior cook at the mess hall in Poston, Arizona, during World War II. Back then he'd won over not a few fans for baking leftover clumps of rice with some sugar to create sweets reminiscent of treats Mari created with cereal and melted marshmallow. When it was rhubarb season, usually in mid to late spring, Jimi's phone would be ringing off the hook for people wanting him to donate his signature pies to the latest temple fund-raiser.

This morning Mas would be treated to apple cobbler. He felt embarrassed because he'd abruptly arrived with nothing in hand. He had come to say hello to Jimi's wife, Ats, as well as to get a handle on the situation in Watsonville these days. Any Nisei or even Sansei, in his daughter Mari's case, knew enough that you needed to bring a six-pack of Coke or even a wilting pot of lilies—hell, it was only *kimochi*! What did the *hakujin* say, it's the thought that counts. And here Mas did not have the decency to come with even one simple thought.

What made matters even worse was that Ats was ill, ill enough for her to be hidden behind her bedroom door.

Atsuko, or Ats, as most everyone called her, had been a bright flame to give balance to Jimi's subdued personality. Her presence had given life to her husband, but now, with her out of the room, Jimi seemed faded, his energy extinguished. Even his ever-watchful eyes looked cloudy. He appeared to not quite remember Mas.

"I live in the house for coupla years," Mas said.

Jimi continued to stare at Mas, as if he were going through some old photos in a tattered album. "How are you connected to Shug Arai?"

Mas frowned. Had this old man really forgotten? Mas knew that he wasn't that memorable, but it seemed like *inaka* folks were better at keeping accounts with the past. "Cousin of cousin."

"Second cousins." Jimi's face flushed with recognition for a moment, and Mas hoped the light bulb had turned on.

"You the one who got in some trouble."

Mas felt his body lurch forward. He hadn't heard about that incident in about fifty years. Since that time, so much had happened—he had moved to Los Angeles, started his gardening business, got married, and raised a daughter. Life brought its share of semi-criminal activity—secret poker games, questionable practices at horse races—but nothing big enough to involve law enforcement, until quite recently. He and Shug, in fact, had an unspoken vow. Never mention it again. So both had buried the youthful indiscretion, the crime committed when they were still in their teens.

"I, I," Mas stuttered, not knowing how to proceed.

Jimi's mind seemed to be clicking and processing information like an old-time computer. "Ats was living at the house at the same time you were."

Eager to change the subject, Mas nodded. "I picked strawberries for you back in forty-eight." He quickly steered the conversation back to his original purpose. "I knowsu your papa, smart guy, start Sugarberry with Shug's papa."

"You didn't know my father." Jimi pushed his half-eaten plate of apple cobbler away. "What have they said about him?"

Mas was confused. It wasn't as if he was being a gossip. It was public knowledge that before World War II, Goro Jabami had been an amateur hybridizer who'd learned about mixing strawberry varieties out in the fields rather than in the classroom.

"My father did the work. That Wataru Arai was just the talker. The money man. He had that house."

Mas kept quiet, so quiet that he could almost hear himself

breathe. In the nearby bedroom, faint moaning. "They make new poison to killsu bugs spreading *yaro* I hear."

"Well, that's news to me," Jimi snapped back. "Can't fix yellows through pesticide. It's a mystery—not sure if it's a virus, bugs, genetics, what."

Someone was knocking at the door and Mas was relieved. He had come here simply for straightforward information, and now he was encountering major curves in the road.

"Jimi, take a look at this." It was the field manager, holding some dug-out strawberry plants.

Jimi ushered the man into his living room, not bothering to introduce him to Mas. Taking out a magnifying glass from a drawer, he examined the strawberry-plant leaves, which were curled and yellowed.

"Shit," Jimi said. "How many?"

"The whole north side."

Jimi covered his face with his brown, callused hands, and Mas felt the enormity of the moment. The strawberry must be sick, he thought, and the culprit must be the talk of the town, strawberry yellows.

Jimi followed the manager out the front door to the porch.

"Tell them to dig them out," Mas heard Jimi say.

The manager, his voice muffled, then said something back.

"Yeah, all of them. Got to get them out before they spread."

The door opened and shut. Jimi, even more broken, shuffled back into his home. He was practically bent over, as if someone had punched him in the gut. He seemed surprised to see Mas still sitting there at the living room table.

Mas immediately rose. He felt like he needed to apologize or express his sympathy in some way. The death of a crop was a death in the family.

"Tell Ats hallo, *ne*," was all he could manage.

After Mas left Jimi Jabami's home, he felt unsettled. Jimi had around five years over Mas, but always seemed much, much older. Perhaps it was because he was the big boss of the tiny strawberry farm, one of the few who actually owned land in Watsonville during World War II. And with people trickling back into town in the late 1940s, laying their heads down in any legitimate space, whether it be in a hallway of a home or the temple sanctuary, Jabami Farms was one of the biggest things going.

Mas wasn't sure what had happened to Jimi's father, Goro. Back then, as they bent over to pull the red fruit off of stems, he heard grumblings from his relatives and the other Nisei workers who now had to answer to Jimi: "Ole man was a lot better. Gave more water breaks. More money for each filled crate."

The workers soon adopted a nickname for their new boss. Jimi Jama, *jama* for interference. For there wasn't a day in which Jimi wouldn't correct their work, tell them they needed to leave more of the stem on the picked strawberry, work from the bottom to the top of their crate.

Ats, however, never complained. She was one of the few girls out there—rumor was that her parents and brother had gone back to Japan on a repatriation boat and she was left by herself in the U.S. She often had to stop and wipe her face from the sweat and steam from her overheated body. Mas half-expected Jimi to come out in the fields and scold her for not keeping a steady rhythm to her picking. The fact that he didn't was definitely an early sign that he was sweet on Ats.

Ats didn't expect much from people, yet she wasn't a typical loner type, either. She was prone to bursts of laughter, which surprised Mas at first, the sharp sounds of a machine gun. It was if she was storing her laughter like rounds of ammunition, and then releasing it at the most unexpected times.

So he understood what Jimi "Jama" saw in Ats. Mas just wasn't quite sure what she saw in him. He was stable, a landowner. But a bit odd as well. He was an only son, an only child, and Mas figured that made Jimi view the world in a solitary way. He'd always just hoped that Ats wouldn't lose her laughter along the way. And, based on the dim house and her closed bedroom, she apparently had.

Mas drove back to the motel, his head full of memories of his days in Watsonville. He had not called either his daughter Mari or Genessee for a day now, and he felt that the past was starting to overtake the present.

He parked in an empty space in front of the motel and walked toward the back, where his room was located. Before he could remove his worn wallet from his pocket to get his room key card, he saw that the door was wide open and the window broken. The window screen had been removed and was leaning against the outside wall.

"What the hell?" Mas mumbled.

A housekeeping cart overflowing with wrapped bars of soap, towels, and tiny bottles of shampoo was blocking the walkway. A thin, dark-haired young woman, wearing an apron and a name tag that read "Cecilia" appeared from the back of the cart.

"You can't go in there, sir. The police are on their way."

Seated in the lobby, Mas mentally went through the contents of his Santa Anita Racetrack duffel bag. Dirty laundry, extra pair of jeans, polo shirt that had been a gift from Mari. Nothing special and definitely nothing valuable. The funeral suit was reportedly still hanging in the closet. Purchased in Joseph's store for short men in Little Tokyo, it had been a bargain back in the eighties.

Must have been a kid, he thought. Why he thought Mas would have anything worth stealing was beyond him.

"Too bad the security cameras aren't working." The maid, Cecilia, brought Mas a Coke from the vending machines. "I'll tell the owner to get that fixed."

A police officer was still up in the room, looking for evidence. Even though this was a minor crime incident, he'd contacted someone from the county's forensics team to take fingerprints.

No need for all that, Mas thought.

"Are you related to the Arais who live in town?" asked

the maid. "I noticed that you had the same last name."

Mas looked up from his Coke, a little surprised. Most maids he encountered weren't nosy like this one.

"My mom used to work for the Arais a long time ago." Before she could finish elaborating, she was sent to deliver towels to a guest on the second floor.

"We'll move you to another room," the desk clerk with the nametag "Scott" said from behind the counter decorated with a giant white flower. He was young, too, maybe not even thirty. He typed something on a keyboard and checked a computer screen. "Perhaps something on a higher floor."

"Don't wanna be on top," Mas said. The motel was at least four floors and Mas didn't relish traipsing up three flight of stairs.

Scott smiled. "You don't have to worry about that. The pool's on the top floor. It's open to guests most of the time, but sometimes it's reserved for private parties."

Hope those parties are not too *yakamashii*, Mas thought, not relishing any noise from outside disturbing his sleep.

The investigating officer finally arrived in the lobby after half an hour. "They're dusting for fingerprints, but it doesn't look too good." He removed a notebook from his pocket and turned to the desk clerk. "About how many people do you have staying here?"

"It's been totally full."

"And no reports about any suspicious visitors?" His voice didn't sound hopeful.

"I did see a truck drive off from the parking lot around ten in the morning. I mean, I noticed it because I hadn't seen it before. It hadn't been signed in."

"What kind of truck?"

"A regular farm truck. Dirt around the tires and rims. It might have been a Chevy. Not sure."

Dirty farm truck, a dime a dozen, thought Mas. Why did the boy find that worth mentioning? Did they know every single car driving in and out of their parking lot?

The officer's radio squawked at his hip. He unclipped it from his belt and responded. He looked at Mas. "Do you have some time now? My lieutenant would like me to drive you to the station so you can answer a few questions."

Once he arrived at the sheriff's station, Mas was led into a small office with a tall bookcase that showcased a samurai sword and dozens of photos. There were photos of the uniformed Robin Arai with men and women of all colors, all dressed in suits. Although Mas didn't recognize them, he had a feeling that he knew exactly what kind of people they were.

There were more photos crowded on an expansive oak desk that took up most of the space. These were people he definitely did recognize: Billy's children, in graduation gowns, multiple colorful leis strung around their necks. An old black-and-white photo of Shug and Minnie at what looked like the Grand Canyon.

The younger Arai entered, her hair still in an immaculate gray-streaked bun. She made a point of closing the door to her jail-cell-size office before taking a seat behind her desk. She gestured for Mas to sit down in a worn metal chair.

"So it seems you're around a lot of action. The Stem

House and now a break-in at the motel."

Mas sucked in his lips.

"Listen, I'll get right to the point, Mr. Arai. I know that you were close to my aunt and uncle at one time, so I'll give you the benefit of the doubt. But it seems like bad luck follows you. And the last thing our family needs is more bad luck."

Mas was transported to the days when he was a school-boy, being scolded by the teacher. He didn't like it then and he didn't like it now.

"Uncle Shug's funeral is over. We have your statement from the Stem House and now today from the motel. We know how to reach you in—" Robin, with the aid of a pair of reading glasses, examined a sheet of paper in a manila folder. "Altadena. McNally Street. So you're all set. Ready to go. Do you understand what I'm saying, Mr. Arai?"

Mas didn't indicate a yes or no, but he knew full well what was going on. He was being run out of his birthplace, the town of Watsonville, California.

CHAPTER FOUR

When he was a boy, Jimi Jabami almost drowned. He went to Monterey to watch the abalone hunters. Wearing large bulky helmets connected to air tubes, the divers disappeared into the deep waters for what seemed like forever. Then, water streaming from their metal heads, they emerged, their woven baskets fat with abalone. Jimi had touched an abalone shell before. Ugly and crusty on the outside, the shell, shaped like a small baseball mitt, held a secret inside: turquoise and green shimmers of light. He wanted to touch an abalone again.

In the rocky tide pools of Point Lobos, Jimi saw his father and another bare-chested man, a strawberry sharecropper, wrestle with an octopus, black ink running down their tanned hands and arms and dripping onto their white, taut stomachs.

Jimi, however, was not as captivated by the slippery, ever-moving legs of the octopus as he was by the sea. He imagined himself like the abalone hunters, walking on the ocean floor, collecting an endless supply of treasures.

So he dove in.

First, the coldness was shocking—Jimi first felt that his heart might have stopped for a second. And instead of seeing the riches of abalone on the bottom of the ocean, he only saw a fog of murky green brownness. The sea water stung his eyes and he cried. When he started crying, bitter water entered his throat, and then when he swallowed, he couldn't breathe. Jimi fought against the water fog, and the fog was winning.

Then he felt arms, slender but as strong as poplar trunks, wrap around his limp body and scoop him out of the water. It was his father, Goro, who later told his friends, the strawberry sharcroppers, "I was not going to let this one die."

It was well known in Watsonville the curse that had befallen the Jabami household. Some said it resulted from the strange union of Goro, literally "Fifth Son," with his wife, Itsuko, "Fifth Child." To have this coincidence was apparently not serendipitous, because the Jabamis lost four girls in childbirth. Two of them before Jimi was born and two of them afterward.

Surprisingly, it had been his father, not his mother, who cried when the youngest daughter died when Jimi was five.

After it happened, Goro went into a local pool hall on Main Street, just across from the river. His friends said he kept repeating that it had been all his fault. That it had been *bachi*, a punishment for something he'd done in the past. Soaked in sake, he returned to his house—to his wife, now with an empty womb, and to his son.

It had been Itsuko who held young Jimi close, ignoring her husband's tears. Her forehead and hairline were wet, as if she'd stepped into a hot, humid downpour. The bedroom smelled strange—on the one hand, antiseptic; on the other, like old *shikko* inadvertently sprayed outside a toilet bowl.

"You," she said to Jimi, "are like Momo-Taro." She spoke of the mysterious boy who had appeared from a giant peach that rolled down a river—a popular Japanese fairy tale. The Peach Boy became the surrogate son to an aging couple with no children. "Only you are our Ichigo-Taro." At the mention of the nickname, even Jimi's crying father sported a sweet faint smile. *Ichigo* Boy. The boy of the strawberries.

Mas couldn't sleep in his new room in the motel. It was the same layout as the first, only the reverse. He had his suitcase back; apparently the thief had used cloth gloves, so there were no fingerprints. Mas didn't notice anything missing, except when he popped out his dentures that night to brush his gums—no toothbrush.

"Sonafugun," he murmured. That young Cecilia or the desk clerk must have dropped it when they were transporting the suitcase.

Uttsuru, uttsuru—he kept waking every hour, imagining someone shattering his windows, shards flying by his head. As he turned his body, the thin sheets fell off the bed. When he finally got up at daybreak, he was sweating and sticking to the plastic-covered mattress.

The first order of business: Once it was a decent hour, go to Minnie's house and tell her that he would be leaving for Los Angeles. Today. He was being kicked out of town by another Arai. Although he didn't like his younger cousin's threats, or at least perceived threats, they were still a good excuse to take off.

After wolfing down coffee and a breakfast burrito at a nearby fast-food restaurant, he headed for Minnie's. When he arrived, he felt his stomach lurch, and it wasn't from the morning meal. It was the large, familiar truck—Billy's—in the driveway, while another sedan was parked in front of

the house. Shug's son was unpredictable and prickly—Mas
didn't know which Billy would appear today.

He rang the doorbell, and an unexpected figure appeared
in the doorway. A white man with white hair and a white
beard. Mas was so startled that he craned his head to check if
he had the right house number.

The man laughed, a giant elf. "You looking for Minnie
Arai's house, you got it."

"Minnie home?"

Who was this *hakujin* man? Should Mas be calling the
police?

"Evelyn took her to the post office. I'm Linus, a friend
of the family. I used to work with Shug at Sugarberry. And
you are?"

Mas cleared his throat. "Mas. Mas Arai."

"Of course," Linus said, extending his doughy hand. Before Mas could prevent it, Linus grasped hold of his hand
and was pumping it for all it was worth. "Shug's second cousin. Yes, I've heard so much about you."

Mas was confused. It wasn't like Shug and he had kept
in touch much during all these years. "Come in, come in.
Minnie will be coming home soon."

There were more vases of flowers throughout the home
—a few fresh as a daisy, others limp and brown.

On the table were stacks of envelopes, white and pastel
colored. Mas knew what they were: cards that held *koden*,
funeral money. And sure enough, a stack of checks and $50
bills sat beside it.

"Minnie's doing all that funeral work. I'm sure you're familiar with it. Something about putting books of stamps in

each thank-you card. A beautiful tradition, I must say."

"Billy?"

"Oh, yes, Billy's resting. He's had a hard time of it, for sure. First his father and now Laila. Shocking. And now the police with all their questions. Minnie's worried about him, and I told her that I'd stay while she was running her errands." Linus then smiled at Mas, as if he were a lovesick teenager. There was something *okashii*, funny peculiar, about this one.

"Anyway, since you're here, maybe I'll be going. You'll keep your eye on Billy, yes?"

Before Mas could protest, Linus headed for the door. He then made an abrupt stop and smiled again before leaving. Mas returned the smile with a slight frown.

Why did Billy need babysitting? He was a grown man. Maybe his whole life he was viewed as a *botchan*, a mama's boy with a silver spoon. Perhaps that's why he had abandoned his wife for a young woman with golden hair. Maybe whatever he saw, he felt he could have, free of any consequences. And now, not only did the *botchan* have to pay the price, but so did everyone else around him.

Mas heard a key turning a lock—Minnie and Evelyn, home from the post office.

"Mas, I'm so glad you're here," Minnie said. "You met Linus, I suppose. I didn't see his car; he already left?"

Minnie didn't wait for Mas to respond. "He's been such a godsend during this time. So has Oily and, of course, Evelyn here. Linus is a longtime friend of Shug. They worked together at Sugarberry. He's a scientist, too."

"I'zu here to tell you I goin'," Mas finally announced.

"To where? Back to L.A.? No, no, you can't go."

"That police lady, your niece, talksu to me yesterday. She don't want me around. Some *dorobo* break into my motel room."

"Oh my God. That's terrible," Minnie said.

Evelyn put down her package and went to Mas's side. "Sit down, Mas. Did you get hurt?"

Mas, who usually got irritated by such attention, surprisingly felt comforted by the two women fawning over him. Minnie rushed over to the kitchen to get him a glass of water.

As best as he could, he recounted what happened to him the day before, especially the encounter with Lieutenant Robin.

"Don't mind her. Her bark is worse than her bite," Evelyn said.

"Actually she's a big softie," said Minnie. "She's just protecting me and my grandkids. And Billy, too. We're the only family she has. After her father died, her mother took off. Married another man and started a new family."

"That's why she's never gotten married herself," Evelyn added. "Works too much."

"Evelyn, hush. I'm sure Mas doesn't need to know that. Anyway, I'll talk to her. Tell her that I've asked you to stay."

This conversation wasn't going in the direction that Mas wanted. He actually agreed with Lt. Robin, that the best plan of action would be for him to return to Altadena. But the two women wouldn't hear of it.

"Beside, Mas, Minnie got you a job."

Mas felt his mouth go slack, loosening his dentures.

"Don't worry. It's just piecemeal, nothing permanent. In the packing shed at Sugarberry."

"You know, so you can spy over there. Be James Bond in the strawberry fields." Evelyn pulled at her shoe-polish black hair and Mas came to the realization that she was wearing a wig.

"You have to stay, Mas," Minnie said. "Or do you have something to go back to in L.A.?"

"If you could travel anywhere in the world, where would you go?" Ats asked. The six of them from the Stem House—Shug, Ats, Evelyn, Oily, Minnie, and Mas—had escaped to Point Lobos during an uncharacteristically warm summer Sunday in Watsonville. It was 1949. All of them except for Evelyn worked six days a week at the apple dehydrating plant, and they were taking a well-deserved break.

It was often Ats who started off conversations with her fanciful questions.

Oily was lying on his back. "Paris. The guys stationed there said French women have the best legs."

All the girls groaned.

"Well, I'd like to go see the geysers at Yellowstone. I hear it's pretty fantastic," Evelyn contributed.

"New York City for me," said Minnie.

"I would go to Egypt and see the pyramids." Ats's ambitious answer surprised them all, and they remained quiet for a moment.

"Yes, the pyramids," Shug agreed.

Ats then turned to Mas. "How about you, Mas?"

Mas never knew how to answer such questions. For him

to travel on a boat for three weeks to San Francisco with only boys his same age or younger had been a huge adventure. He couldn't imagine any more overseas adventures in his lifetime.

"C'mon, Mas, come up with an answer." Evelyn pulled at his shoulder, causing Mas to grimace. Evelyn was constantly touching him, punching his arm, playing with his shirt. He didn't know if this was the American way of getting a man's attention; if it was, it was a wonder that anyone was getting married at all in this country.

Mas didn't want to be coupled. Not this time in his life, before he was twenty. He didn't want a woman to tell him how to dress, what kind of work he should be looking for. He didn't want to be trapped in a tiny sedan with a box of *onigiri*, rice balls wrapped in seaweed, driving up a winding road to see the geysers at Yellowstone.

He wanted to pack all his belongings in one bag and set out for the road, feeling free to take a *hirune*, a nap, underneath an oak tree, to feel the hush of twilight, to smell the end of a day. He didn't feel the need to be responsible for anybody else in his life. He didn't want to be confined in a box, led by a leash. Maybe someday, but not yet.

Now, some fifty-five years later, Mas was back in the same place as he was in his late teens. He could do as he chose, although now there were ties to Mari and Genessee. But with Genessee, it was just thin twine that could be untied at any time. There were no promises of a future.

"No," he told Minnie. "Nuttin' waitin' for me."

They heard a noise in the hallway. Billy appeared, wearing the same clothes as the day before. His afternoon shadow was nearing full-blown beard status. The short hair on top of his head looked like a patch of weeds. "What is he doing here?" he asked no one in particular.

"Billy, don't be so rude."

"We're trying to convince him to take a job at Sugarberry. To be our spy."

Billy's dark eyes rested on Mas's face. "You should," he said. "To find out who killed Laila." He then turned and went back to the darkened hallway.

"You weren't kidding, Minnie. He's sure not doing well." Evelyn shook her head.

"I tell him to go back to work. Work always helped Shug feel better."

"Shug was a hard worker," Evelyn agreed. "And you were, too, Mas. You two seemed like you were everywhere, hauling tomatoes, picking lettuce."

"They used to call them the Two Kilroys, because they seemed to show up everywhere. You two were connected at the hip."

Mas almost cracked a smile. Shug and he would often compete on how many crates they could fill. They were eighteen, nineteen years old, with energy to burn. Maybe seeing how Sugarberry did things wouldn't be a bad idea. Mas suspected that the strawberry cooperative would pay him at least enough to buy a few meals. Nostalgia again reared its powerful head, and before Mas knew it, he had agreed to spend at least one working day at Sugarberry.

The late afternoon fog was starting to move in on the

Jabami farm. Jimi was up on a ladder inspecting the leaves on his apple trees. He knew that yellows was something that could be passed from one fruit to another, but somehow he felt that everything near him was getting poisoned. The orchard, as far as he could see, was fine. It would be a good autumn harvest. For a moment, Jimi felt an ache of sadness. He wished he would be there to see the branches weighed down with ripe red apples, to pull down a ready piece of fruit and hear the stem snap free, to bite into the skin and white meat, juice pooling on his chin.

One year all his grandchildren, from faraway places like Minnesota, Texas, and even Sweden, were here in the orchards for Ats's and his fiftieth wedding anniversary celebration. It wasn't that long ago. Ats was *genki* then, laughing with the children and even chasing them through the apple trees.

Jimi had first laid eyes on Ats in the Arizona camp, in the mess hall where he helped mix goopy freeze-dried eggs and mashed potatoes with water.

She wasn't particularly pretty, but then she didn't seem to care that she wasn't. That was the first thing that drew Jimi to her. She wasn't like the other girls in camp, who were constantly primping their hair in spite of the relentless desert winds that would loosen and blow wild the most perfect of curls.

She wasn't afraid to be alone. In fact, one day, hours before dinner, he saw her sitting alone in the mess hall, a book in her hands. He never saw her with her parents, but then, most of the teens ate with their friends and not family members.

Under the guise of cleaning the tables, he got close enough to see the title of the book that she was reading.

The Stranger.

"Any good?" he asked, a gray wet rag in his hand.

"Okay. Not really my cup of tea, but Miss Everett says people need to stretch themselves sometimes."

Jimi didn't quite understand. How do you stretch yourself by just sitting there and reading?

'Where you from?"

"Block Twenty-one."

"No," he said. "Back home."

"Salinas."

"Salinas, we're practically neighbors." Jimi added that he was surprised they hadn't met at a regional Junior YBA event.

"My parents aren't religious," she said.

"Farmers?" he asked.

"You like asking questions."

His face colored. "No, actually," he stumbled over his words.

She carefully placed a bookmark in her copy of *The Stranger* and got up from the bench.

Don't go. I'm sorry. I will let you be, Jimi wanted to call out. He didn't care if the girl didn't talk to him. As long as she stayed in that spot the whole afternoon. But apparently he had intruded on her solitude and she, like a migrating butterfly, escaped out the screen door.

Days later, he saw her walking with Shug Arai. *Why always the Arais?* he thought to himself. *Why did the Arais always seem to win the prize?*

Jimi's luck changed when they returned to the West Coast after the war. He didn't know how it happened, but the butterfly flew to him and had stayed with him ever since.

Reentering the house, Jimi heard moaning and hurried into the bedroom. The caregiver, wearing nurse's scrubs, was at Ats's bedside.

"Active today, Mr. Jabami," the caregiver said. "She keeps calling for you."

"Ats, I'm here." Jimi clutched at his wife's hand. It felt so fragile. All her nails had turned black and were splitting like dried-out bamboo.

"More morphine?" he asked her, pressing down on the remote to administer the painkiller. Only so much, a few milligrams worth, was allowed to safely drip down into Ats's bloodstream. *One day, this will all be over,* he silently promised his wife. In Jimi's packing-shed refrigerator, carefully wrapped and hidden beside jars of strawberry preserves, was that special package. Waiting, waiting. For when the time was right.

CHAPTER FIVE

Yes, we can! Yes, we can!"

"*Sí, se puede! Sí, se puede!*"

Mas tried to pull up his collar to be less conspicuous as he walked through the protest line. Apparently he didn't have to worry. No one seemed to notice him.

He had parked the truck along a dirt road about two blocks away. Seeing the line of protesters assembled in front of the Sugarberry driveway, he didn't want to take any chances for his Ford to get vandalized. It may have looked like Mas was *doudemonai*, didn't care one way or another, but he'd actually carefully chosen each newly fused spare part from the multiple junkyards he'd visited.

The crowd thrust hand-painted signs toward cars passing on the street.

SUGARBERRY, NOT SO SWEET FOR WORKERS

KEEP OUR FAMILIES SAFE

There was a woman with dark, wavy hair who seemed to be leading the charge. She had a bullhorn and was not afraid to use it. "Shugaberry shuuugacoat no mo! Shugaberry shuuugacoat no mo!"

As Mas got closer, he could hear the chant more clearly. "Sugarberry, sugarcoat no more! Sugarberry, sugarcoat no more!"

Mas didn't care for chants, whether it be at a political

protest or in a Buddhist temple. He also didn't care much for *urusai* activists who polluted the open air with their noise. When he first moved down to Los Angeles, the gardeners were embroiled in a labor conflict of their own. Told to join a union, the gardeners said no, without the chants. They had grown their businesses through their own sweat and tears, sometimes booking one lawn job immediately after another. They asked their customers to hang their monthly checks from the clothesline; there was no time to knock on kitchen doors and wait to be paid. *We are independent businesses*, they claimed. Many of them had spent three years locked up in a dusty camp and were sick and tired of institutions telling them what to do. *We are our own bosses.*

Mas entered what looked like a newer extension to a warehouse. Plain white, it was purely functional, with no decoration in sight. A secretary at one of the metal desks assisted Mas and gave him a nametag, directing him to the packing shed across the way.

Sugarberry was one of the oldest strawberry cooperatives in Watsonville. Farm cooperatives allowed growers to become members so they could share in patents, knowledge, and distribution. The cooperatives originally were started by Japanese immigrant farmers in the early 1900s. Back in Japan, they'd learned that not only two heads, but sometimes three, four, or maybe a dozen were better than one. As a result, farmers came together cooperatively to share capital to survive cash-flow troubles and even to stabilize prices, which could go up and down from week to week. In Watsonville, the Sugarberry cooperative was also able to take advantage of refrigerator cars, so even before the Great Depression, its strawberries made it all the way to New York City.

Mas had done his share of strawberry packing in the past. Now his brand-new supervisor, Carlos, was directing him to a seat next to a conveyer belt. Each packer was assigned a large box of glossy strawberries, which they packed into smaller clear plastic clamshells, making sure that the less attractive ones went first in the bottom. Once packed, the clamshells were snapped shut and placed on the conveyor belt to be packed again into larger boxes.

Mas's co-workers, mostly middle-aged women, looked at him curiously as he slid on the silicone gloves.

"*Nombre?*" one of the older women asked him.

Mas knew enough Spanish to answer. "Mas."

"*Más?*"

"*Más?*"

"*Más?*" It seemed that a number of the women found humor in his name.

"*Más, por favor?*" More, please.

"*Más agua?*" More water.

"*Más tequila?*" More tequila.

Finally he couldn't take it anymore. "*No Más!*" he said. *No More!* The room erupted in high-pitched laughter.

He had survived the new-employee initiation. In fact, he did more than survive. He passed with flying colors.

At eleven-thirty, they stopped for a half-hour lunch break, and Mas's coworkers made a beeline for the catering truck that had parked next to the protesters. Apparently the protesters were also on a lunch break.

A man was in an intense debate with the woman with the bullhorn. "Listen, Rosa, I wasn't going to protest at a man's funeral, okay? I don't care what he might have done. I'm not going to do that to a dead man's family."

"Even though he was using genetic engineering to create a new strawberry?"

"You don't know if he was or not."

"Well, it had to do with yellows, that's for sure."

"We'll find out next week."

"But by then it will be out. Laila wanted us to stop it before it was introduced."

"What are we stopping? We look like fools, Rosa. Nobody understands our message, because we don't really understand it."

"I don't know why you're like this. You pour cold water on everything. The protest at the funeral and now. . . ."

"And you should be glad we stopped you. The little support you have would have been gone, like that." The man snapped his fingers.

"Just come tonight." She handed the man a half-sheet flier, which he promptly dropped on the ground.

"Two *machacas*," the catering truck worker called out from a small window.

As Rosa left to pick up her taco order, Mas picked up the flier. "Work for Food Safety for All," it read, and it listed a downtown address. The day and time of the meeting: tonight at seven p.m.

Mas stuffed two carne asada tacos in his mouth, one after another. He could eat soft tacos one-handed, his favorite method of eating. Wiping his hands on his jeans, he was back in the nondescript office in just a few minutes to fill out some employee paperwork.

As he carefully entered his Social Security number on a form, he felt someone staring at him.

It was Jimi Jabami, wearing a Sugarberry windbreaker. He looked a tiny bit better than he did yesterday when he'd heard the terrible fate of his strawberry crop.

"What are you doing here?" Jimi didn't even bother to sound friendly.

"Workin."

"Working? In the packing shed?"

Mas nodded.

"I thought you were going back home."

Mas pushed up his reading glasses. He had said nothing of his schedule to Jimi. "Just spendin' a few days here. *Inaka, inaka* feelsu good."

Mas felt like a fool saying such nonsense, especially to Jimi, who had a strong nonsense detector.

Jimi balled up his fists, and his fish eyes seemed to bulge out even more. *Why did the old man care if I work here,* wondered Mas. He didn't call the shots at Sugarberry. Or maybe that was the point.

Mas resumed filling out his form, but he knew Jimi wasn't quite finished with him. Through a window he watched Jimi march up to Carlos in the parking lot, probably trying to get to the bottom of his employment.

When he returned to the packing shed, Mas wasn't surprised when Carlos came up to him.

"I fire?" he asked, almost relieved.

"You kidding me? You know how to do hard work," Carlos said. "You have good hands. Workingman hands."

Feeling self-conscious, Mas stuffed his hands in his pockets. "Jimi Jabami talksu to you."

"Jimi gives me a piece of his mind everyday. I can't blame him this time. You heard about his crop?"

Mas nodded.

"And I think these protesters have him a little on edge. They tried to organize the workers at Jabami Farms last month. The union lost by two votes. That doesn't have much to do with Sugarberry, that's what I told Rosa, you know, the woman with the megaphone. We are just the distributors. The farms are all independent. She doesn't listen to me. Has an axe to grind with Sugarberry, that's for sure. She's no fan of Shug—you're related, right? She hates... well, hated him."

Mas's coworkers, all full of tacos, were trickling back to the conveyor belt.

"For me," Carlos concluded, "Shug was hero, a genius. With their patents and new varietals, Everbears is becoming a contender. Sugarberry needs something to keep up with them and all the others. Without innovation, we are dead in the water."

The seven o'clock meeting for Rosa's group was being held in an historic building on Main Street. Mas recognized it from his teenage days of wandering around downtown Watsonville and was astonished to see that it was still standing. The city had been hit hard by an earthquake in the 1980s. Mas remembered the photograph in *The Rafu Shimpo* newspaper that he got in the mail most every day. Piles of bricks in the place of the two-story buildings he remembered.

Rosa was already speaking in front of a small crowd of twenty-five people in folding chairs. Mas opted to stand at the back of the room next to a table that held a coffee maker and stack of paper cups. "We are dedicating tonight's meeting to a dear, dear friend, Laila Smith." Rosa's voice cracked; it was obvious that the two women had been close.

"Laila cared about you, the worker and student. She devoted . . . no, she risked her life for us. During the methyl bromide battles, Laila, as a student at UC Santa Cruz, fought hard to ban that fumigant. She didn't grow up here, but her heart was here. She cared about clean water and air, about preserving our best for the next generation."

Mas was here because Carlos had mentioned that the protesters did not look at either Shug or Sugarberry that favorably. Did their animosity fuel the demise of Shug? Was his killer right here in their midst? He scanned the crowd. He thought he recognized a few of the pickers he'd seen working the fields at Jimi's farm. There were also a couple of young *hakujin* people, looking deceptively shaggy and dirty on the outside. In the back row, sitting by herself, was a young brunette, her thin arms firmly crossed. Familiar, Mas thought. He squinted his eyes. It was Cecilia, the maid at his motel.

"So it's our turn now. We need to step forward. All the corporate brass, co-op leaders, and big growers will be at the strawberry commission meeting next week. Two new strawberry varieties will be announced, varieties that were built on the back of our labor. In addition, there are rumors that Sugarberry has been using genetic engineering in these new berry varieties. We've all heard stories of GMOs, of radiation in our food, of the crossing of fish cells and strawberries. We can't let that happen.

"The local media will be there, and we need to be in full force to show them that we don't want our food soiled by radiation and biogenetics. Our leaders in the past sacrificed their lives so we can work under healthy conditions. We can't go back in time."

The meeting dragged on and on, with various people talking about "logistics" and strategies. Determined to see if anyone would mention Shug's name, Mas tried to stay alert, but his eyes kept drooping shut, even while standing. Seeking some kind of help, he went to get a cup of coffee. Cecilia must have been feeling the fatigue, too, because she was right behind him.

"Hello, Mr. Arai," she said.

"Hallo." Mas poured at least a tablespoon of sugar into his cup.

Cecilia wasn't wearing her name-tagged apron. "I didn't know they grew strawberries in Los Angeles," she said.

Mas frowned. Again the girl seemed to know too much about him.

Before he could respond, someone tore the steaming Styrofoam cup from his hand, splashing coffee onto the concrete floor.

"Mom! What are you doing?" Cecilia was aghast.

Rosa, the attacker, placed her knuckles on her hips. "I heard you are one of them." She was about two inches taller than Mas and leaned so close to him that he could see the fine lines around her mouth.

Mas waited for clarification.

"Them. The Arais."

"Stop it. He's not from here. He's from L.A. He's a nobody."

Mas, for once, felt very happy to be called a nobody.

"Doesn't matter, he's still an Arai," she said to her daughter and turned back to Mas. "Your people killed Laila, you know that?

"She was getting close to the truth. Billy knew that. I kept telling her, blood is thicker than water. Watch out. She thought Billy was different. Not like the father. But look what happened to her.

"She found out something the night she died. What Shug Arai was hiding about the announcement they were going to make next week."

"Shug already dead." This woman was *kuru-kuru-pa*. How could Shug have revealed something from beyond the grave?

"These secrets could speak after death. A trail of deceit," Rosa spat out. Mas could hardly follow what she was saying.

"She was going to talk to Billy about what she discovered. I begged her not to. It was so earth-shattering that she couldn't even tell me over the phone. 'This will change the world,' she told me. 'When we blow this out of the water, we'll be on every website and on the cover of every magazine. It'll be that big.'

"The morning after she tells me this, she's found dead in an Arai greenhouse."

"You'zu so sure, why don't you go to police?"

"Oh, yeah, you people have that covered, too. Lieutenant Robin Arai. But I've gone above her head to the sheriff's county headquarters. They know now. They know not to trust any of you Arais. All you care about is money. Status. Yourselves. Your precious family."

Mas was too stunned to reply. All the air in the old building seemed to have seeped through the cracks in the walls and ceiling. He tried to breathe, but he could not.

"Nothing to say now?" Rosa continued. "Well, just wait until we get to the bottom of this. I've found out who was helping Laila with analyzing Sugarberry's new variety, and it won't be long before I know, too."

Mas had heard enough. Leaving the coffee-stained floor and the angry Rosa, he turned and walked out to get into his truck and hightail it out of there.

"Mr. Arai, Mr. Arai," he heard a high-pitched voice on the other side of the crosswalk.

Hugging a drawstring bag to her chest, Cecilia crossed the street to reach Mas. "I'm so sorry," she said. "My mother is intense, but she doesn't usually go this far. She's just so messed up over Laila dying and all."

"*Orai, orai*," Mas said. He was now practically used to Watsonville folks taking out their sorrows on him.

"Hey, can you give me a ride to the motel? I don't think my mom's going to be ready to go anytime soon."

At first Mas thought that Cecilia didn't have much in

common with her mother. But he was wrong. They both like to talk. A lot.

"Laila was her best friend. They did everything together. Mom took it hard when Laila got together with Billy Arai. She said it was sleeping with the enemy. Plus Billy has a wife and kids, you know. I went to high school with Billy's daughter, Alyssa. She was so tight with her dad, you know, before all of this."

Mas tried the best he could to pay attention to the girl's sing-song banter. He opened his eyes wide and glanced in his junkyard side mirror, a former fixture on a semi truck in a past life. Behind him was a pickup truck, its right headlight dim, as if it was close to burning out.

"I kind of got why Billy was with her. Laila could win guys over with her looks. She got pretty much everyone and everything she ever wanted. I mean, she was rich herself, although no one really knew. That's why there's no funeral in Watsonville—her parents in Monterey took away her body. They pretty much barred Billy and my mom from going to the service. My mom wanted a memorial service here, but she wouldn't work with Billy on it."

Cecilia finally took a breath when they were at an intersection about a block away from the motel. "I hate to say this, but, in a way, I think Laila deserved what she got."

Mas's foot almost slipped from the brake pedal. What a *hidoi*, severe, thing to say.

Noticing Mas's reaction, she quickly clarified, "I'm not saying that I'm glad that she's dead—just that it doesn't surprise me. She never thought about anyone else's feelings."

She gestured to the corner. "Can you let me out here?"

It just occurred to Mas that it was late for a maid to be reporting to work.

"I study in empty rooms there sometimes. My neighborhood is way too noisy at night. The manager doesn't know about it, so I have to sneak in."

Mas stopped the truck and waited for Cecilia to get out.

"Thanks for the ride," she said, picking up her bag from the floor of the truck.

The girl jumped out and ran to the side of the motel. In his side mirror he saw the reflection of a a pair of headlights, one bright and one dim. Before he could open his door to get a better look, the truck made a sharp U-turn and disappeared down the street.

Why was Mas Arai hanging around in Watsonville, when he was clearly a city boy? Jimi had spent most of the day following Mas and his strange, beat-up Ford truck. In the *inaka*, pick-up trucks were ubiquitous, everywhere. But ones like this, fashioned via Frankenstein-type surgeries, indicated a man who didn't care what other people thought.

And he claimed that he was taking a break by working in the packing shed at Sugarberry. Didn't make any sense. No sane man vacationed in a packing shed. Suspicious, Jimi had asked the packing shed manager what was up with the hiring of Mas Arai. Turns out that Minnie Arai had made a special request. Of course. Jimi had heard that she couldn't believe that Shug died of natural causes. No one was listening to her. No one except perhaps Shug's second cousin.

As Jimi returned to the house from his truck, he passed four stone markers. Four buried baby sisters. This Mas Arai may be trouble, he murmured to his four sisters. *But don't worry, don't worry.* He wouldn't let anyone, especially an Arai, keep him from what he needed to do.

CHAPTER SIX

Cecilia's offhand comment about Laila put Mas in a bad mood. For as much as he thought Laila's involvement with Billy was wrong, Billy himself was more to blame. He was the married one; he was the one who had broken his vows. If anyone could be blamed for Billy's marital woes, it would have to be Billy.

All Mas knew was that he didn't want to be played as a chump. He didn't know exactly what Billy's game was, but it clearly wasn't a game with any set of rules. Back in his room, Mas didn't bother to turn on the light. He sat in the darkness at the minuscule desk, feeling his knees almost touch the wall. Rosa's words had soaked in, more than he'd wanted to let on at the time. *Your people killed Laila*, she'd said. Was there any truth to her accusations? And what about Billy? He'd taken Mas into the Stem House after having a fight with Laila, and he'd conveniently kept all these secrets from Mas and maybe from the police. This all had to stop. Now.

Outside Mas heard the sound of high heels against the vinyl walkway. The stride was quick; this one was in a hurry. During his stay at the motel, he'd often heard the slow, unsure steps of a drunken trucker or the sliding of children's tennis shoes. This sound was different. Mas lifted the edge of the plastic curtain. It was Cecilia, in a tight animal-print dress and shiny black pumps. Not studying clothes, that's for sure. As she darted up the staircase that went up to the fourth floor, he wondered who she'd dressed up for. There was a pool up there, wasn't that what the desk clerk had said? Cecilia, however, did not look like she was going for a late-night swim either. Perhaps she was on her way to one of those private parties.

Whatever it was, Mas knew he wasn't invited, which was more than fine by him. He just feared being disturbed by the syncopated beat of electronic music or perhaps yelling and laughter by young men and women. Thankfully, however, all he heard was the hum of the wall heater, which lulled him blissfully to sleep.

The next morning, Mas called Minnie and found out that Billy had gone to work—his first day back since Laila was found dead. Whether he liked it or not, Mas's next destination had to be Everbears. He couldn't just sit there as suspicions dangled like overripe fruit. They had to be picked before they dropped and destroyed anything that was potentially good.

As Mas drove south on Highway 1 to Everbears, he felt like he wasn't in Watsonville anymore. It turned out to be more than a feeling, for he soon passed a sign that said, "Welcome to Moss Landing." With its oceanfront location and humble pier, Moss Landing was a sleepy former port town. Mas was surprised that a strawberry distributor would be located in such a place, but maybe Everbears wasn't your typical farm co-op.

Instead of a nondescript prefabricated building, Everbears occupied a converted warehouse clad in aluminum siding. A tangled metal sculpture, apparently in the form of a strawberry, was a clue that it was not co-op business as usual in this place. Across the street was a fenced empty lot with a sign declaring the property was the future location of Forever Resort. A resort? In Moss Landing? Resorts were for Hawaii, not for Pajaro Valley.

The Everbears' signature logo, a white strawberry flower that would eventually turn into a juicy piece of red fruit, was everywhere on this one block, even on the sign for Forever Resort.

Inside, a large white paper globe hung from the lobby ceiling to light the room. It looked like a Japanese lantern from a summer festival, quite a difference from the harsh, bare fluorescent bulbs at the Sugarberry offices. The floors were made of bamboo. Mas detected a scent of something musky emanating from a pot on the receptionist's desk.

While the receptionist was finishing up a phone call, Mas took a look at a framed magazine article on the wall. "High-Tech Whiz Sets His Next Sights on Berries," the headline read. Within the story was a photograph of a pasty-faced young man with long, stringy hair.

As Mas continued to wait, Oily walked into the lobby. He was wearing a polo shirt and khaki pants. "Mas, what are you doing here? Thought you were spying on Sugarberry."

Minnie must have told him, Mas figured. "Lookin' for Billy."

Oily smiled, but somehow it looked to Mas like there was no genuine feeling behind it. "Sure thing. I'll take you to his office."

They went through a door in back of the receptionist area and walked down a narrow hall that also had a stylish bamboo floor. They finally came to a door with a sign that said "Research and Development."

"He's in there," Oily said, turning as if to leave.

"How about you?" Mas had expected Oily to come with him.

"I can see that this is family business. Best if I leave it to you two to hash it out."

Mas opened the door and found himself in a white room, one side lined with desks. On the other were industrial refrigerators and a table with a microscope and blender. On the wall between the two sides was a long whiteboard covered with writing arranged in charts that looked like family trees.

Billy was sitting at one of the desks, speaking to someone whose back was turned to Mas. As soon as Mas walked in, Billy rose from his chair. "Mas."

Shug's son did brief introductions. "This is the owner of Everbears, Clay Gorman. Clay, this is Mas Arai. My father's relative. He's in town for the funeral."

Clay Gorman was wearing a long-sleeve gray t-shirt. He looked like the delivery boy instead of the boss. Clay didn't bother to extend his hand, so Mas didn't offer his. Instead, he slightly bowed his head, as if Mas was straight from Japan.

"So we're on the same page on this, right, Billy?" Clay said, completing his conversation. Mas narrowed his eyes. The skinny neck and shoulders, Mas had seen those before. The mourner at Shug's funeral who was right in front of Mas at the incense line.

Clay awkwardly bowed again and left the room.

"Sorry, he's got some social issues," Billy explained. "Lived in Tokyo for a while and is crazy about things Japanese, anime, *go*."

Mas nodded. Oh, the boy was one of those. Likes to talk to computers and robots more than human beings. Mas continued to take in everything in the room. On Billy's desk sat about a hundred strawberries on a white cutting board, all cut in half. Each berry was tagged with a number and name.

"Whatchu doin'?"

Billy quickly blocked Mas's view of the board of strawberries. Strange.

"I thought you were working at Sugarberry."

"I was," Mas said. "Been meeting some *omoshiroi* people. Like dis woman Rosa." Mas didn't like her, but he could honestly say that she was interesting.

"Rosa Ibarra?" Billy's face turned dark. "I think *she* was the one who hurt Laila."

Mas shuffled in his workboots. Yet she was saying precisely the same thing about Billy.

Billy folded his arms. "Sometimes I thought that she was in love with Laila. Ever since we've been together, Rosa made it her mission to go after me and my family."

"She say you and Laila *kenka*," Mas said, and then realizing that Billy might not understand, he repeated himself in English. "You fight."

"Yeah, we fought. Especially recently."

"You fight dat night." The night Laila was killed.

Billy sat back at his desk, clearing the way for Mas to see his severed strawberries. "She told me she'd seen my father before he died. He accused her of stealing his computer, of attempting to get his scientific secrets." Mas then remembered that Minnie had mentioned that Shug had just purchased a new computer, which apparently had replaced the stolen one.

"She'd been following my dad. He hadn't been going to his consulting office—he'd been going to Linus Verdorben's place in Castroville. Strange place next to his father's old body shop and closed-up gas station. Verdorben has some fields over there, too. The Masao test plants. Laila said she got hold of a strawberry plant—took one up to UC Davis to have some friends do some tests. The day she died . . ." Billy's voice wavered, "she was supposed to show me the results. She said it was important. I told her I didn't want to hear it—my dad's funeral was the next day, for God's sake. I just took off in the middle of our fight. Went to the liquor store to get some beer and drank for a while. Then I felt a need to go to the Stem House. Just for old times' sake. Dad always said his best years were in that house."

"We have some good time," Mas agreed.

Billy lifted his chin up and Mas noticed that his eyes were still bloodshot. "He always spoke highly of you, by the way. Always did."

Mas pressed his lips together. He wasn't here to fish for compliments, just to uncover the truth.

On the desk was an Everbears mug, from which Billy took out a pencil to play with. "So I never found out what Laila wanted to tell me. I've been going through her things, her papers. The police have her computer. And then I found her cell phone in her car. That's when I heard these threatening calls on her voice mail."

Mas shivered. It was as if the temperature dropped.

"It was a man's voice. Saying that he would hurt her if she stayed in Watsonville. I don't know why she didn't tell me or report it at the time. But she did save the messages; she must have taken the threats seriously." Billy held the sharp end of the pencil out, like a miniature saber. "I dropped off Laila's phone at the sheriff's office this morning. They'll be checking her records. They will get this sonofabitch."

Mas didn't care much one way or the other. Maybe that's why Billy was spilling his guts to him, because Mas really didn't have any strong opinions when it came to Laila Smith.

"Nobody understands, you know. My kids. My family. Her family. Her friends. But we had a special connection."

Oh, yah, Mas said to himself. In his seventy-odd years of living, he knew all about so-called "connections." They usually led old men down a path of destruction. Billy must have read Mas's facial expression, because he shook his head.

"No, it wasn't like that. I mean, yes, she was gorgeous. And young. But it was much more than that. She was so, so—alive and curious. Open about life. It was starting to rub off on me, too. We talked about going to Latin America, Chile. See how other cultures dealt with food production. Maybe write a book together."

Book? *Kuru-kuru-pa*, thought Mas. There was no doubt that Billy had lost his mind.

"I was going to tackle the science part of it; she, the political side. Our party politics didn't match, but we were both committed to getting the best food to the most people. Really. It's really her passion that got her killed."

Billy's eyes took on a glassy sheen and Mas, embarrassed by any sign of emotion, looked down. He noticed something else sticking out from the mug on Billy's desk. A white plastic knife with the words, "Masao," clearly written in Shug's hand. "*A-ra*—" he couldn't help to exclaim. This was a marker from the missing strawberry plants next to the Stem House. The ones that Shug had bred and named after Mas.

Billy frowned and followed Mas's gaze. "It's not what you think," he tried to explain. "I mean, yes, I took them that night when I left the Stem House. But it's only because they were my father's. I wanted something of his."

Mas was unconvinced.

"I was curious. I mean, Laila was talking like these plants were revolutionary. I don't know who the parents were for these plants—yet." Billy gestured toward the chart on the whiteboard. "Every variety has a family tree, an initial mother and father."

He pointed to the sliced strawberries tagged on the cutting board—apparently those were the Masaos. "Anyway, just by doing a special taste test, these don't seem to be anything special. I mean, they're sweet, very sweet, but the meat doesn't hold up."

Mas let out a deep breath. He was disappointed to hear that his namesake was just like him. Totally unspectacular.

Billy wasn't completely finished. "There's something about this strawberry, though. You can't tell by just looking at them."

Masao felt a little sick. What did Shug try to hide, and did Laila discover his secret? Who made the threatening calls to Laila? Perhaps there was a connection between Shug's death and Laila's. Maybe finding out what happened to Laila would provide new information about Shug.

Mas's head felt like it was spinning. "I needsu to go," he told Billy. He stumbled out of the laboratory and finally into the lobby, where he saw a familiar-looking teenager talking with Oily.

"Okay, I'll check on that, too. Maybe the server's been compromised," the teenager said, and Mas immediately recognized the voice. It was the same one that had challenged him at Shug's house. The owner of the Impala hardtop.

Mas scurried out of the lobby and got into the Ford. What was a no-good teenager doing at the Everbears headquarters, talking to Oily? Didn't make any sense. He decided to learn more.

Mas moved the truck to the other side of the street next to a strawberry stand. As he waited, he drained the last bit of coffee and threw the crumpled disposable cup onto the passenger side floor. It was probably ten minutes before the boy got into his Impala and left.

Mas followed, staying at least one car length away, which was difficult as the cars became fewer and fewer on the country road. He was about three car lengths back when the Impala slowed and then came to a complete stop. It then backed up suddenly until the Impala's rear bumper almost touched Mas's truck, forcing Mas to brake. The boy leapt out and stalked over to Mas's side window. "Okay, so what the hell do you want?"

Mas sat frozen behind the 1970 dashboard, which he had installed some years ago.

"C'mon, this pile of junk, I can see it a mile away. I know you were following me since Everbears." The boy was wearing old-fashioned thick-framed glasses, the kind that

Shug used to wear.

Mas rolled up the window as far it would go, about an inch from the top of the window frame. He attempted to shift to reverse, but another pickup truck had come from behind and was honking its horn.

"Pull over," the bespectacled boy ordered before running back to his car. They both moved their vehicles to a dirt embankment next to a strawberry field.

Grasping onto a crowbar from behind his seat, Mas was ready for anything that would come. He came out first.

The teenager, seeing Mas with his weapon, began to laugh. "Cool it, old man. I'm not going to do anything to you. I just wanted to know why you were following me." He put his hands in his hoodie sweatshirt. "I've seen you at Mister Shug's house. You a relative? You kind of look alike. Around the eyes."

Mas didn't know if the teenager was insulting him or not, but decided to give him the benefit of the doubt. "Heezu cousin. Of cousin."

The boy's face softened. "Uh, sorry then, man. We all went to the funeral. Even my brother and he doesn't like to get out of the house much. My great-grandpops used to work for Mister Shug's old man. That was a long time ago."

The boy handed him a business card. Victor Duran, DuranDuran Recovery, it read. You Lose It, We Find It. Mas had one of his own, ORIENTAL LANDSCAPING, but he doubted it would hold any water with this Duran boy.

"It's my brother's and my company. He's an information security expert. Went to Cal State Monterey and worked at Clay's high-tech company before it got bought out. Got downsized, so we decided to go out on our own. I'm the people person, so I meet with the clients."

People person? Mas shuddered to think what the brother was like.

"So why you following me?"

"Tryin' find truth. About Shug dyin'."

The boy's face, which was dark, turned a shade of olive green. "Who you talking to, the cops?"

Mas shook his head. Yes, he had been talking to Robin, but she was officially off the case. "Minnie ask me to help." And Billy had, too, in his roundabout way.

"How's she doing, by the way? Haven't talked to her in a couple days."

"Lotsu goin' on."

"Yeah, I've been thinking of Mister Shug. I saw him getting the newspaper the day he died. He always called me Ichi—that was his nickname for me. You know, for Number One. Said that I was smart. Not too many people have called me smart." Victor's face grew tender for a moment. Mas was surprised.

"I was going out for a morning appointment. Wish I'd been around. Maybe I could have done something, but I don't know what."

"Your brotha home?"

"Yeah, but he's kind of useless with stuff like that. Just stays in his room with his computer. Our *bisabuelito*, great-grandpops, even has to bring him food; he won't eat otherwise. But Mister Shug was worried about something. All about the announcements of the new varietals next week."

Shug was right; this Ichi was smart.

"Yeah, about a week ago, he actually hired me. I mean, I usually don't do work for Sugarberry, since, you know, Everbears is one of their competitors. But Mister Shug is almost like family. And it was personal. His laptop was stolen from his house. He had a computer Lo-Jack on it, but he said he didn't want to involve the police.

"So we said that we would handle it. At first the thief didn't turn on the computer. It's like they knew that Mister Shug had some kind of tracker on it. But then it was turned on for about an hour. Enough to see that Mister Shug had wiped clean the hard drive. Through the tracker we located the computer out by Moss Landing harbor. I'm sure it was eventually tossed in the water."

He pushed up his glasses, which were starting to droop down his nose. "One thing they didn't know was that something else was on. A webcam. My brother was just able to download the saved image."

Mas straightened his back in anticipation.

"I can't say anything, okay. I can't get involved, you know, for professional reasons. But I can show you." Victor went into the Impala's trunk and took out a laptop. Opening it, he clicked a few keys and rubbed a mouse pad. Bringing it over to Mas, he said, "This is what my brother got."

The image was a bit dark, but Mas could make it out.

A face—boxy and framed by thinning gray hair. Oily Takei.

During his lifetime, Oily Takei had gone through three

marriages, which didn't surprise Mas in the least. During the short time Mas lived at the Stem House, he'd witnessed the Casanova in action. He usually started things off with some undivided attention, some compliments, and then flowers. Next came picnic lunches with *onigiri* that Shug's mother had made, along with some teriyaki chicken. Then before you know it, the girl was hanging on Oily's arm, a nice new brooch on her dress collar. After a month or two, the whole cycle would repeat itself, much like planting new crops on the same piece of land.

Oily was smart enough not to practice his romantic moves on the girls living in the Stem House. They weren't going anywhere for a while, and he couldn't deal with bumping into a former lover in the hallway on his way to the bathroom. But it was obvious, at least to Mas, that Oily had long carried a torch for Minnie.

Minnie, with her cat-eye glasses, was not Oily's type, and Oily, being all brawn and little brain, was not Minnie's, but perhaps that was the attraction. She was a flavor that he could not easily try, and Oily was all about new flavors.

One day they all went down the coast to go clam digging at Pismo Beach. They brought shovels and pails, rolled up their pant legs, and went to work at low tide.

The clams clanged as they tossed them in their pails, and at one point, Oily called Minnie over to his.

"Look," he said.

The curiosity was a clam with a fat siphon extended like an excited *chinko*.

"Oily." Minnie turned bright red. It was obvious that he wanted to stir things up with her. Shug then made a joke and all of them laughed. Minnie's honor was immediately restored.

Shug at that point had been playing it cool. But once it was clear that Oily had his sights set on Minnie, Shug finally moved in, drooping shoulders and all, and he prevailed. Their wedding had been simple, Mas gathered. By the wedding day, he'd moved to Los Angeles and contact, unfortunately, became more sporadic. Now with funerals, the gang had more opportunities to be reunited.

Mas wondered if he really knew anything about Oily as he was now. Some things most likely hadn't changed since their teenage days. Oily was no friend of loyalty; in fact, he'd been the first to leave Sugarberry for Everbears. And more recently, according to the Duran boy, he had recruited Billy to work for the competition. And as with his work, Oily liked to keep his options open in his personal life. After Wife Number Three left him, he must have been lonely. With Shug out of the way, the path to Minnie was free and clear.

"Can't say anything to him," Victor said. "He's our main contact at Everbears. You know, our bread and butter."

"You'zu in a bad situation," Mas said.

Victor nodded. "My *bisabuelito* thinks we should take this direct to Mister Oily. My brother says let sleeping dogs lie. As for me, I don't want to think the worst of Mister Oily. He wouldn't do anything against Mister Shug, would he?"

Mas honestly didn't know. Oily talked a good game, but from personal experience, Mas knew that his old friend had a tendency to flip-flop allegiances. Victor, looking at his vibrating cell phone, said he had to get going.

Mas wasn't quite finished with him. "One more thing—you'zu help Shug with sumptin else?"

Victor frowned, his thick eyebrows now dark slashes above his glasses.

"Minnie findsu it."

The teen sighed. "It's not illegal or nothing. My friend was getting rid of one of his guns. Shug said that he needed it. For protection. He had this feeling that somebody was out to get him."

"Mister Jabami," said the caretaker, picking up her purse as she walked from Ats' bed to Jimi, who was standing in the bedroom doorway. "I hate to say this, but I need my money tomorrow."

Jimi nodded, embarrassed that he'd had to ask her to wait on her payment for a week. He was expecting that the money from this week's harvest would have come through by now, but that was before the yellows. The second mortgage on the house and the loans on the farm equipment all had been pressing down on him, squeezing him, causing him sleepless nights.

He knew that he probably should have spoken to their children, but they had their own lives in faraway places. No, it was his responsibility to figure this out. And he had. The mortgage insurance policy would take care of the farm and the house, and that's all that really mattered. The children wouldn't sell the property, he knew. Most likely, it would be the divorced daughter in Texas who would come out and move in. Her children were almost all grown.

Sometimes in the middle of the night when the moon was full, Jimi would walk the perimeter of his house alongside his strawberry fields. He'd check their leaves, touch the berries, and talk to his fruit. *Gambare*, he'd encourage them. Hang in there. The winter had lasted too long this season, but he'd ask them to persevere. Then he'd come through his gates into the front yard, where the lemon tree gave shelter to his sisters. Sometimes he'd imagine them as babies, their fat thighs and skinny eyes. Even though they were newborns, in his mind they would be dancing, laughing, saying full sentences to one another. They were free and would remain free, as long as the Jabamis had their land.

So the morphine tablets, purchased from a drug dealer by the Pajaro River, were there for Ats. She was close to death anyway, so no one would suspect. Figuring out his own demise was a bit tougher, but Shug had helped immensely. Jimi had everything in place. But then this new Arai had come into town. Once he was gone, the plan could proceed. This Arai just needed an extra push out the door.

CHAPTER SEVEN

giant stone rolled down a creek, building more and more speed as it came closer. The soft edges of the creek bed were being destroyed, chunks of moss-covered soil flying and hitting Mas's face and neck. The rock hit the trunks of five cypress trees, almost knocking them over like bowling pins. Smashing against a boulder, the stone cracked open, releasing the severed head of Oily Takei, which then began to float upward, growing larger and larger.

Mas jerked himself awake, finding himself practically mummified in the motel sheet. Could Oily have killed Shug? He worked for a competitor, Everbears. He himself had said strawberry yellows threatened the whole industry. Did he steal Shug's secrets to save his own company? Or perhaps it was more personal, longtime jealousy plus a desire for Minnie after all these years.

It was eight o'clock, early but not that early. He had already called Mari over the weekend to tell her that he was staying. Now it was time to make another call.

"Hello."

"Hallo."

"Mas, it's good to hear your voice. Mari told me you'd be staying up there a few more days. How's everything going over there?"

Genessee Howard's voice was like tiger balm without the

overwhelming menthol smell. Her voice literally warmed Mas's creaky joints, soothing, relaxing.

Mas, as best he could, told Genessee what had happened these past few days. Laila's dead body. Shug's mysterious death. Minnie's call for help. Spying at Sugarberry. Strawberry yellows.

"And now Oily," he said, concluding with the discovery that it had been their childhood friend who had stolen Shug's laptop. "I'zu need to come home."

Genessee was quiet for a while and Mas wished she would fill the silence with "yes, yes, Mas, come home."

But instead he got this: "You've got to stay, Mas. They're family."

Family? Genessee never seemed that particularly happy with hers.

"Never underestimate the importance of family," she reminded him.

Feeling recharged after speaking to Genessee, Mas took a shower, brushed his gums with a new toothbrush he'd purchased from the drugstore, and combed his wet hair. He felt, for once, optimistic. Maybe doctors would find that Shug actually had a weak heart, all along. That Laila's killing had been a random incident—perhaps a hungry vagrant or drunkard who wanted his way with her. Nothing involving strawberries. Mas knew he was just fooling himself, but it felt good to try.

He watched television for a while, getting recaps of what

was happening in basketball and baseball back in Los Angeles. Then a knock at the door.

Without even looking, Mas knew he wasn't going to like who was behind the door. Robin Arai, out of her uniform and out of her hair bun. Her shoulder-length hair was in slight disarray, which made her look like an everyday person.

"I won't blame you if you don't want to talk to me," she said.

At least the lieutenant had realistic expectations.

"I'm not here in an official capacity, but a personal one."

Mas, halfway curious, gestured for her to enter. Closing the door behind her, he turned off the television.

"I'm off the Laila Smith case. Conflict of interest. Arturo Salgado has officially taken over." She stood awkwardly by the wall air conditioner.

"They fire you?"

"No, no it's nothing like that. I'm still working at the station." Although out of her uniform, Robin still stood as straight as pole. "They traced the threatening phone calls to Laila. It came from a landline at a dorm at San Jose State. The dorm where Alyssa lives."

Mas had to concentrate for a moment. Who was Alyssa again? Sounded familiar.

"My niece. Billy's daughter."

Mas knew nothing about her, other than her smooth, shiny face and long hair. Before he could fully absorb what Robin was telling him, she quickly interjected, "She didn't do it. But sheriff's detectives are going to question her today and I'm trying to get her a lawyer. I'm not supposed to contact her, but I tried. She's not answering her phone and she

has too many messages in her voice mail. I keep telling her
to clean it out."

"Her motha?"

"Colleen? Well, she's not quite available. She hasn't been
available for a while. After Billy moved out, she had a nervous
breakdown. She's been in and out of mental facilities. She
insisted on coming to Shug's funeral, but I think seeing Billy
was too much for her, and she checked herself in again."

Robin then swallowed, slowly and deliberately. "So, you
see, it has to be someone else to tell her to wait for a lawyer.
Do you understand what I'm saying, Mr. Arai?"

Mas did but didn't want to.

"Here's a map to her dormitory. It's on campus." She
took out a folded computer printout from her purse and
handed to Mas. He accepted it, begrudgingly. He didn't
want to drive anyplace within Watsonville, not to mention
fifty miles away. In order to hit the 101, he'd have to travel
through the twists and turns of Hecker Pass.

"Please, Mas, as a favor to the family."

Ah, *shikataganai*, Mas thought to himself. This all could
not be helped. All he knew was the next time he talked to
Genessee, he'd tell her that she was very wrong. Family is
very overrated.

After Robin left, Mas put on his work boots and windbreaker. In all honesty, he doubted he'd be able to find Billy's
daughter. Young people rarely stayed in one place; they were
always on the go. But he saw something in Robin Arai's eyes

that he had seen before: fear. She was scared for her niece, and she was most likely scared because she cared for her so much. That sentiment Mas actually understood.

So he'd go to San Jose, because he said he would. Other than that, no guarantees, that's what he told the policewoman. As he started the Ford's rattling engine, another truck started as well.

Where was this Arai going? First he'd been visited in the early morning by the other Arai, the police officer who was out of uniform. What were they conspiring about?

Jimi's eyes were red, his eyelashes crusted with yellow sleep. He had spent the night there at the side of the parking lot, with Mas's strange-looking monster of a truck in plain view. He'd brought a thermos of coffee, as well as a fresh coffee cake that he'd made. The caretaker was with Ats; he made some excuse that he had to go out of town on business.

He followed Mas from Green Valley Road to Airport Boulevard to finally the 152, Hecker Pass. Heading east—maybe Gilroy or San Jose? Jimi drove past strawberry fields, past the cemetery where most of Jimi's father's ashes were buried. The remaining ashes had been released in the hot winds of Arizona, sixty years ago.

Jimi remembered his last conversation with his father. "No, *da-me*. Don't come too close," Goro said from his hospital bed in Poston.

Jimi didn't care what his father said. He wasn't afraid of tuberculosis. He wasn't afraid to die. In fact, he wanted to enlist in the Army like some of the other young men in camp. When his mother, Itsuko, found out, she just turned her head toward the barracks wall.

"*Nagakunai,*" Goro said. It won't be long. He had been placed in the Poston Hospital a month ago.

"Listen," he said. "Listen." Goro wasn't one to say much, but he spoke now. He spoke about how he dreamt of strawberries. Red colors of all different shades, scarlet, blood red, wine-colored. The minuscule seeds pleating their plump skins.

"I have a special strawberry, one that I was experimenting with Wataru Arai," he said in Japanese. "It is a strawberry like no other. But we cannot let the Arais have it all. Part of it belongs to us, the Jabamis."

What can I do? Jimi asked. They were in camp, locked away. He had seen Wataru Arai working in the victory gardens, his shirt sleeves rolled up and his skin tanned and weathered like tortoise legs. There were no strawberries in that desert garden. Strawberries needed the coastal air. Wataru Arai had not brought strawberries to Poston.

"No, no," Goro whispered. He tugged at Jimi's elbow. His breath smelled strange, like unripe bananas. "We hid the plants. Wrapped them up, special barerooted. Stem House, basement."

That had been two years ago. Barerooted strawberry plants stored in a cool place could last one, two months, at best. Jimi squeezed his father's hand. "Papa, it's okay," he said.

"No, no." Goro was more adamant this time. "The strawberries were saved. They were saved." Before he could say more, a nurse, originally from San Juan Bautista, stopped by.

"Your father should not be so agitated."

Jimi tried to argue with her, and Goro even attempted fruitlessly to get up.

"It's okay, Papa. You can tell me tomorrow."

"I named it Taro," he said. "After you. Remember? Strawberry Boy."

Mas circled the dense streets of downtown San Jose. One-way streets everywhere, lined with older multilevel office buildings. Mas felt like he was traveling in a maze with no ending point.

Mayotta. Hopelessly lost.

He felt himself grow angrier and angrier. Why had the woman police officer sent him to do this work?

Finally finding a place for the Ford in a parking structure, Mas followed the signs to San Jose State University. He had been here once before, to see one of Shug's friends participate in a judo tournament. But that was more than half a century ago, and much—but not everything—had changed. He saw the same redwood trees, looking a little worn after all this time, as well as palms stretching above the red-tile slanted roofs of Tower Hall. Dark-haired young people were swarming all over the campus like ants seeking to conquer their landscape.

Robin had been good enough to include a computer printout of the map to Alyssa's dormitory, a twelve-story building that looked like it could hold at least five hundred people. How could he find Alyssa amid all the other long-haired Asian coeds?

After he made a couple of missteps, a student who seemed to have pity for Mas pointed him toward a desk on the second floor of the building.

"Alyssa," he said. "Lookin' for Alyssa Arai."

A young woman who could have been Alyssa's twin, aside from wearing oversize red-framed glasses, furrowed her eyebrows.

"I'zu relative. Mas Arai. Family emergency."

The girl bit the end of a pen and then dialed a number on the desk phone.

"Alyssa, there's someone's here for you. A relative. He says it's an emergency."

Within five minutes, Alyssa appeared from a long hallway. She didn't even bother to say hello. She pulled Mas into a corner away from her bespectacled twin. "What are you doing here? Did something happen to my grandmother?"

Mas took Alyssa to the other side of the lobby. The student receptionist continued to keep an eye on them, but at least they were far enough that she couldn't overhear their conversation.

"Robin tole me to come ova. Police comin' to talksu to you. Don't say nuttin' to them. Robin gettin' you a lawyer."

"A lawyer? But why?"

"Police knowsu all about the te-le-phone calls you make to Laila."

Alyssa began to blink furiously. "I had my boyfriend call. I wanted to scare Laila off. To tell her to move out of Watsonville. But we only did it a couple of times. Then my boyfriend said he didn't want to be a part of it. We aren't together anymore."

Mas was ready to leave, but the girl apparently wanted to continue talking.

"I didn't do anything to Laila. I didn't bash her head in. I was sleeping over my aunt's house when she was killed. The police can ask Robin and my brother."

Why did Alyssa feel the need to spout out her alibi to me? Mas wondered.

"You don't think the police will want to talk to my ex-boyfriend?"

Naturally they will, Mas thought.

Alyssa quickly read his face. "No, that won't be any good. He's really pissed at me. I don't know what he'll say to the police."

Apparently more frightened by the prospect of dealing with her ex-lover than with a murder charge, Alyssa started to tremble.

"Wait for lawyer," he said, and she nodded.

"It's all his fault, you know. My dad. If he had his midlife crisis or whatever by just buying a sports car, we wouldn't be in this mess."

They then heard voices from the courtesy desk a couple of men in bad suits were talking to the receptionist with the red glasses.

"Rememba, don't say nuttin'," Mas repeated to Alyssa before going out a side door.

Jimi got back in his truck. He placed his wrench back in the glove compartment. He was a stickler about returning things to their proper place. The nut that he'd removed from a screw, he could have tossed it away, but he instead put it in his jeans pocket. Maybe he'd place it in a jar when he got home. A souvenir, at least before Jimi and Ats's last days.

It had been easy with an old Ford truck from the 1950s. No electronics or computer circuit boards to deal with. Being a farmer, Jimi had serviced more tractors and pickup trucks than he cared to remember. But in this case, he wasn't fixing a vehicle, but breaking it down.

He didn't know whether he should follow the Ford on its way through Hecker Pass. Hecker Pass was winding like an angry snake on the side of a cliff. He wondered how the truck would crash. Over the ledge, falling, falling hundreds of feet below. Or perhaps it would be like that winter Olympics game, the bobsled. The truck would shoot down the winding road at record speeds and then crash into the side of a mountain, maybe even bursting into flames.

Jimi remembered traveling on Hecker Pass when he and his mother Itsuko returned from Poston. The loss of his father had been devastating enough in camp, but somehow it felt worse after they were released. At least inside, all the people seemed to prop them up, whether they liked it or not. But now free, they were unanchored, untethered. It was as if their small family was floating away from each other, never to meet again.

Itsuko never recovered from Poston. She spent her days outside beside her four stones. It was as if she felt every loss in her life, over and over again.

"It was harvest time, the fields full of red strawberries. We had to leave them all. I wonder if anyone picked the strawberries," she said, remembering when they were forced to leave their Watsonville land. Luckily they had an attorney who had taken care of the property taxes during their absence. But nobody was there for the strawberries. The Taro, Jimi wondered. What had happened to the Taro strawberry?

One summer night, the night of Watsonville's first Obon festival after camp, he could not sleep. Most of the Japanese, at least the Buddhist ones, were at the temple, dressed in cotton *yukata*, clutching and waving fans and cutting into the hot, humid night air with their sharp hand movements. Even though they lived miles away from the temple, Jimi swore he could hear the beat of the large drum, the *taiko*, with wooden sticks, pounding, pounding. He told his mother he was tired. Which he was, but there was also something else.

The Stem House was completely dark, the window shades down like closed square eyelids. The Arais, cornerstones of the temple, would be at the dance, which meant Jimi could finally pay the Stem House a visit. Armed with his flashlight and a leftover spare rib, he went through the unlocked front door.

The Arais' black poodle, Kuro, started his insane barking, but as Jimi thought, the spare rib was a perfect bribe for the dog's silence. Jimi himself was a dog lover, with two miniature collies at their farm house, but he had no affection for Kuro. Anything that the Arais cared for, he could not.

He swept the walls and furnishings with the beam of his flashlight. Their family portraits, their smiling faces seemed unending. In Jimi's case, there were more family members in the ground than above it.

What had Jimi's father said? The plants had been hidden in the basement. A couple of turns around the house and he spied a door cut into the side of the back stairs. He turned the glass doorknob and yes, found the steps leading to complete lower darkness. A perfect place for hibernating strawberry plants. He descended and circled the floor with the flashlight. He saw a dirt outline of squares and a lone crate, an old-fashioned one hammered together by hand. Jimi kicked it to the side and noticed the label. Jabami Farms, it read, with the painted image of a juicy strawberry adorning the label's right side. He knelt down and picked up something on the ground that spilled out from the old crate. Strawberry roots, shriveled up like dead spiders, on the verge of disintegrating to dust. There must have been crates full of them at one time. And now they were gone.

Mas noticed something *okashii*, again funny peculiar, with the Ford right before he got on the highway. The truck lurched forward, and the front brake squeaked louder than usual.

Okashii.

But then, there were a lot of *okashii* things with the truck. Although it was built in 1956, Mas had squeezed in a 1970 dashboard, compliments of a junkyard in Monrovia. It was a neon-yellow Chevrolet set, sawed off to fit the Ford and fastened together with black duct tape. Mas steadied the truck onto Hecker Pass. Driving over the pass on his way to San Jose had been a bit of an ordeal; the truck shook and jerked like it was on drugs. Now, he figured that coming back to Watsonville would be a little easier. He'd be going downhill. Steep inclines, sharp, angled turns, fun for billiard players, but a challenge for old-man drivers. Mas knew he would have to pay attention.

The sun was starting to go down and the diffused light bothered his eyes. Beyond the two-lane highway, beyond the clumps of giant redwood trees, was a ledge to nothingness. The sky, a glowing gray, filled with the rolling fog.

Mas pulled at the steering wheel at an almost ninety-degree turn and pumped on the brakes. Another pump and another pump. Instead of slowing, the Ford seemed to be picking up speed. Mas fought with the old truck and leaned forward to put all his weight on the brake pedal. But the pedal was on the floor and there were no signs of deceleration.

In spite of the high speed, everything inside seemed to go in slow motion as the Ford went off the road. The crumpled coffee cup on the floor floated up as if it were in outer space. The pens and mini-flashlight jumped up from the cemented coffee cup, the makeshift ashtray danced in the air. The car visor flapped like the wings of a seagull. And then the truck rolled once or maybe twice. Mas felt the cinching of the seat belt around his belly and then he was flying, flying. An awful roar of the Ford's exterior scraping against asphalt and rock. And then everything went black.

CHAPTER EIGHT

The first thing out of Mas's mouth was, "Whathappentomytruck?" His voice sounded strange and muffled, as if someone was pressing on his neck.

"Mr. Arai, please relax." The nurse gently pressed Mas's shoulders back on his pillow. "Don't try to speak."

Mas's head felt woozy and his throat was sore. There was some kind of beeping machine next to him. He focused on another figure in the room and practically jumped.

Mas frowned. "Hekillme?"

Oily's mouth fell open.

"He's heavily medicated. He doesn't know what he's saying." Minnie was also in the room, which Mas now figured must be in a hospital. He couldn't see her, but that definitely was her voice.

"*Chotto, chotto,*" he called out to her, and she obliged. He tugged at her sweater sleeve and warned, "Watchout, watchout."

"Watch out for who?" Minnie looked puzzled.

"It may be better if you both leave now," the nurse said to Minnie and Oily. "Let him get some sleep."

It was so dark. But it wasn't night. Black, black, black. Then orange flashes in a distance. Smoldering, suffocating fire. The flames roared forward, licking the Hiroshima train station.

"Riki!" Mas yelled out. "Kenji!" And finally, his best childhood friend, "Joji!"

Where were they? Where were they? Mas grasped at his neck. Why couldn't he breathe? The air was getting thin, and he kept scratching at his throat.

Suddenly a figure of shining white appeared through the ashes. Shug, but instead of the drooping shoulders, muscles the size of Superman's.

"Shug, what are you doing here?" Mas gasped.

"I've come to save you." Shug's voice sounded strange; it echoed through the hollow station. Where were his childhood friends, where were the passengers? And where was the fire?

The ground then shook, the walls giving way, more dust and debris falling, falling. Got to get out, got to get out.

"Mr. Arai! Mr. Arai!" The nurse called out.

Mas pried his eyes open.

In his hands was his tracheotomy tube, extracted from his throat. Mas tried to swallow, but his mouth felt destroyed. Raw.

"You weren't supposed to pull out your tube," the nurse said, annoyed. "Now we'll have to put that back in." She left to get the doctor.

Luckily, the doctor determined that Mas could probably breathe on his own, with the help of an oxygen tank. So the hole in his throat was cleaned and bandaged and a simple plastic tube laced underneath his nostrils and held in place by his earlobes. Still not ideal, but more comfortable. At least he could speak better now, which he did when Minnie finally returned to the room.

"I see Shug," Mas told him. "In my dreams, I see him."

Minnie smiled, if you could call it a smile. Just a faint upturn of her upper lip. "He's in my dreams, too."

"Heezu all white, shiny like a star. Muscle all ova."

Minnie chuckled, covering her mouth. "Are you sure that it was Shug? What you're describing sounds like that man on my cleaning detergent, Mr. Clean. Maybe the TV was on while you were sleeping."

Why did the Shug in his dreams say that he had come to save them? Save them from what?

Minnie sat in the padded chair next to Mas's bed. "One time I dreamt that Shug was on a stage, like in a music concert. He was surrounded by cheering young people. It was quite a scene. But then he fell off the stage right onto his head. He was wimpering for me to help him. I couldn't reach him." Minnie then sniffed loudly and Mas regretted bringing up the dream. He tugged at his hospital wrist band.

"You gave us quite a scare, Mas." Minnie rested her pocketbook on her lap. "And I think you hurt Oily's feelings. He didn't want to come back here."

"Heezu the one, Minnie. Heezu the one who killed Shug."

"Now, now, you've been through a lot. Don't you worry; we've called Mari and the whole family is coming up tomorrow, after your son-in-law finishes work."

Mari, Lloyd, and the grandson. *Oogoto.* Chaos. No, no, no. Also Mas knew how difficult it was to travel with the toddler. And with the regular baseball season starting, Mas knew that Lloyd was overburdened with work. Not much his son-in-law did was impressive to Mas, but being connected to Dodger Stadium was actually something to brag about— even though he was a groundskeeper and not a player or executive. "No, no, *da-me*." Mas tried to pull himself from the bed with the metal handrails. His lips were bone dry; when he touched them, flakes of skin fell off.

"Mas, relax, please relax." Minnie attempted to push him back on the bed.

"You call Mari. Tell her don't bother to come."

Minnie sighed and got out her cell phone and, using her address book as a reference, dialed some numbers. She apparently got Mari on the other line, because she started to give a full medical report: "Uh, huh. Concussion. He's got a few scrapes. And they had him on a breathing tube, but he's off of it now. Yeah, yeah."

"Lemme talk."

"Here he is." Minnie held the cell phone to Mas's ear.

"Dad, how are you doing?"

"Don't come ova."

"What are you talking about? Of course we are coming. I've booked our flights. We will be there tomorrow night."

Mas pulled the phone from Minnie and held it to his other ear. "No, no, I'm *orai*. You all gotsu *yoji* to do."

"Don't talk about work. You've gone through a serious accident. You can't be there on your own."

"Not alone. Minnie here." Mas looked at Minnie and she nodded her head. She took the phone from Mas's hand.

"Mari, don't worry. He obviously doesn't want to burden

you, but we're here for him. I have time to watch him and after he's discharged, he can stay with me." Minnie then turned
her back from Mas. "Yes, well, it's been totaled," she said.
"Yes, completely."

What was totaled? Was it what Mas feared it to be?

"Do you want to say anything more to her?" Minnie
asked Mas.

Mas shook his head. He felt frozen. Coldness spread
down to even his fingertips.

Minnie flipped her phone off and took a deep breath.
"The Ford's gone, Mas," she said. "It's no more."

Mas remembered when he first laid eyes on the Ford. It was
a dealership in South Pasadena, where a former gardener,
Yak Fujii, had started to work part-time as a salesman in the
1950s.

There had been a recent run on Ford trucks, not to mention the Chevrolet—usually pronounced She-bu-re by Kibei,
men who were born in the U.S. but raised in Japan. For the
undiscerning, there was little difference between the Ford and
Chevy—the same blue-green exterior, the shade of the bottom
of a moldy swimming pool. Yet there was a difference.

There was only one 1956 Ford truck left in the dealership, the last model for the season. While the She-bu-re's
white grill evoked a skeleton wickedly smiling, the Ford's
look was more *shibui*, restrained. More Japanese in an Amer-
ican-made body.

What Mas also appreciated were the Ford's running

boards, which were positioned right below the doors—easier
to step in and out when you were only five feet two. Mas
went back and fourth with Yak a couple of times, then it was
a done deal. The Ford was his.

After all these years, the Ford was his only surviving com-
panion. It was there, carrying Mari as she jumped onto the
back bumper and held onto the tailgate as he eased into the
driveway after a long day's work. It was there, working, when
Chizuko passed away from cancer. It was there when their
dog died. His Ford had survived being stolen and stripped.
But it had not survived Hecker Pass.

The loss of the Ford was more painful to Mas than the
tube that was shoved down his throat. Who would he be
without his fifty-year-old trusty sidekick? What car would he
drive? The room seemed to move and shift. Mas felt sick to
his stomach. He asked for a bedpan and vomited over and
over again.

Jimi Jabami had never seen anything quite like it. The truck
turning over not once, but two times. The neon-yellow seat
shooting out with its passenger tied to it like a rag doll. The
hunk of metal squashed like an aluminum can. And the
sound. The sound was incredible. Worse than anything he
had ever witnessed in a junkyard.

Jimi had parked his truck behind a grove of redwoods.
Soon other cars and a semi stopped, blocked by the smashed
Ford pickup. A couple of people had run over to Arai, who
was attached to the ejected seat. They were trying their cell

phones, but there was no reception. The trucker then got on his CB radio; authorities were on their way.

Jimi waited until the paramedics arrived, unbuckled Mas from his yellow throne, and moved him to a gurney. He saw no sign of a coroner, which meant one thing: Mas Arai was still alive. He had nine lives, like that stray country kitten Ats had adopted. The kitten had been run over by a tractor—every single bone in its trembling body should have been crushed, yet it lived. It mewed its way through ten more years.

This stump of a man had survived the atomic bomb, Jimi then recalled. There was something in his genes that kept him going and going. Other than sporadic visits to the temple, Jimi was not a religious man. He did believe an eye for an eye, however. There was something—or someone—who wanted to keep Mas Arai alive. So maybe the thing to do was not necessarily seek to destroy him, but keep him distracted, at least until it was over.

When it was time to pick up Mas, Minnie didn't come alone. Oily stood behind her, his lower lip extended like a sumo baby's.

"I can't have you two feuding if you're staying with me, Mas," Minnie said, her purse hanging from her arm.

"He's the one who's accused me of being a cold-blooded killer of my best friend. I don't appreciate that." Oily's voice shook.

"Listen," Minnie interrupted. "I don't care how you do it—but you two work this out. Right now. Before we leave.

I'm going to the cafeteria for a cup of coffee." She disappeared out the door.

Mas was dressed in Shug's pants and shirt, because his had been cut open by the medics. He leaned against the hospital bed. He wasn't going to be the first one to talk.

"Minnie told me that you think I stole Shug's computer," Oily finally said. "Well, you're right. I did."

Mas was surprised by Oily's easy confession.

"We've been worried about the progress of Billy's variety, whether it would stand up to Sugarberry's strawberry. We figured if we just had a look at Shug's patent before it was filed, we'd know what we'd be up against."

"Who's 'we'?" Mas asked.

"My boss. The president of Everbears. Clay Gorman."

As he spoke, Oily's whole body seemed to grow a bit smaller. "We're kind of in trouble, Mas. Overextended ourselves. Grew a little too fast in too many different kinds of berries. And then Clay's vanity project, the Forever Resort. He wants to use that as a tool to attract venture capitalists. We're in the red, and I'm not talking strawberry red. I should have retired a long time ago, but I need to keep working to support all my ex-wives."

Mas breathed in and out, still feeling a soreness at the base of his throat.

"Anyway, Shug's computer was wiped clean, as you probably heard. I should have known as much. But I told my boss that I would at least try."

"Where'su computer now?"

"Dropped it into the bay," Oily said. "I've already confessed to Minnie. I told her all about it. I wouldn't do anything to Shug. He was like a brother to me."

They two men stayed silent for a while. Nurses walked back and forth, responding to beeping machines in other rooms.

"Friends?" Oily put out his hand.

Mas accepted the handshake. Inside, however, he resolved to always keep one eye open when Oily Takei was around.

CHAPTER NINE

As a rule, Mas didn't like to stay in anyone else's house but his own. There was a Japanese expression, *ki o tsukau*, literally "to use up your feelings." It used up Mas's feelings to have Minnie waiting on him hand and foot. It used up Mas's feelings to wear Shug's old clothes and have Minnie wash his dirty underwear. It used up Mas's feelings to have her cancel her bridge classes to spend time with him. Pretty soon, Mas wanted to shout, *stop using up my feelings, it's wearing me out!*

He determined that he needed to get better as fast as possible before he was all used up.

After a meal of pork roast and sticky rice, Mas and Minnie looked through old photo albums over cups of instant coffee. She gave him a magnifying loop to take a closer look at the faces.

Mas stared at one of the photos. It was a black-and-white image of Shug as a teenager, with another Nisei boy around the same age. In Shug's hand was a bat marked by unusual writing burned into the wood.

Minnie looked over his shoulder. "Oh, do you know who that is?" she said, pointing to the boy next to Shug.

Mas shook his head.

"Fibber," she said. "Fibber Hira, Hira. . . ."

"Hirayama," Mas completed Minnie's sentence, surprising both her and him. How did he know this? Of course, he was the baseball *senshu.*

"Yes, that was it. Fibber Hirayama."

"Bigshot baseball in Japan. For Hiroshima Carps. My hometown." My Japanese hometown, Mas silently corrected himself. Mas was already in California when Fibber made it big as a Carp, but the news had spread across the Pacfic Ocean onto the pages of the local Japanese newspapers in the 1950s. Fibber had only been an inch taller than Mas, but he was known for his hustle.

"Eventually came back to California. Fresno. Became a teacher, some kind of educator, I think."

Moving the magnifying loop over the page, Mas stopped at the bat that teenage Shug was holding. There were the familiar markings—it said "Poston," in both English lettering and Japanese *katakana.*

"Dis Shug's daddy's bat."

"Yes, that's the one my father-in-law carved in camp. After the war, he kept it in the greenhouse, used it as his cane. We told him he should get a proper cane—even bought some for him, but he never used them. Too vain. So instead he'd keep the baseball bat in the greenhouse, you know beside the door. He said he carried it around to scare the chickens away, but we all knew that he needed it. To lean on."

"So datsu why you'zu put it in coffin."

Frown lines appeared on Minnie's forehead. "What?"

"Bat right next to Shug."

"You know, I didn't even notice it. I know we put in the grandchildren's drawings and things. Their teddy bears. I haven't seen that bat in years."

"No, the bat in there."

"Well, the last time I saw that bat was in the green-house. . . ." Minnie stopped herself and pulled at her neck-lace. "Well, anyway, if you say so, Mas." The light from the living room lamp reflected off her bifocals. Mas knew she didn't believe him. But he was sure of what he saw.

Later that evening, Mas sat outside on the stoop. It was times like this he wished he hadn't quit smoking. To hold the cig-arette between his index and middle fingers, to inhale that blast of nicotine and let out the smoke—it would cast the whole world in a new light. Instead of the clear, sharp lines that didn't forgive, the smoke would make everything a bit blurry, somehow more digestible.

Mas didn't have help from to-ba-co right now. But he did have a bump on the head that made certain details fuzzy, including the pain. The pain had changed from being sharp jabs to a dull ache.

A car roared up the street and parked in front of the neighbor's curb. Mas saw a line of cars in the driveway—a torn-up camper, a red Toyota truck, and a silver Oldsmobile.

Victor was still wearing the same glasses and hoodie when he noticed Mas sitting on Minnie's porch.

"Hey, you," Victor said. "Mister Shug's cousin. I don't think I got your name last time." The teenager jumped over the begonia bush dividing the two properties and walked over to Mas.

"Mas. Mas Arai."

"Más? Didn't know you had some Mexican blood in you."

Mas didn't respond. The joke was old the first time he heard it.

"So, anyway, Miss Minnie mentioned that you got into an accident. Totaled your truck, huh?"

Mas nodded. He'd forgotten about the Ford for a moment.

"Sorry, sorry."

Mas gestured to the boy's sedan. "Me own an Impala. Long, long time ago."

"For reals?"

Mas nodded. "Same model. Getsu hot in summertime."

"You bet. You can fry an egg on the hardtop. Actually I've tried it."

Mas laughed. Just what a snot-nosed boy would try to do. "Eat it?"

"Yeah, I ate it. Kind of runny, but I ate it." Victor looked back at the Impala. "That was my *bisabuelito*'s first car when he came to Watsonville."

"Mine was second passenger," Mas said. "Studebaker first."

"Hey, you want to meet my great-grandpops?" Victor said abruptly, as if it just occurred to him.

Whatthehell, Mas thought. Did he have anything better to do?

The Duran house felt familiar. It was a house with no women, just like Mas's. The few pictures on the walls were edged with dust. A couple of posters, either featuring men with guitars or women in bikinis, were taped haphazardly, motivated by impulse more than aesthetics.

The elder Duran was sitting in a wheelchair at the kitchen table, filling out a sudoku grid. Mas had tried sudoku a couple of times and found it unsatisfactory. So what if you got all the numbers arranged in the right slot? Unlike poker, blackjack, or even solitaire, you could always change your answers. No self-respecting gambler would go for those rules.

"*Bisabuelito*, this is Shug's cousin, Mas. He's from L.A." He then identified the old man Duran as Miguel.

Miguel pulled out the other chair in the kitchen and motioned Mas to sit. He faced was as pockmarked as the moon and he wore a neatly trimmed mustache. Victor remained standing but didn't leave.

"Shug's cousin, huh?" Miguel finally said.

"Second cousin."

"Where you from??

"Born here. Watsonville."

Miguel narrowed his eyes. "I never seen you before."

"Papa and mama take me ova to Japan as soon as I could walk. Two older brotha, too. Came back afta World War Two."

"He lived in the Stem House, *bisabuelito*," Victor interjected.

Miguel seemed to almost jump in his chair. "When?"

"Coupla year. Til 1950."

"No kidding. We probably passed each other in the streets. Do any farm work?"

"Work for Jimi Jabami."

"My family took care of the Stem House at first during World War Two. My father don't write, so I was writing the family all the time."

Mas had always wondered who had taken care of the house during the war. He had figured a *hakujin* lawyer, not a farmworker whose roots were most likely in Mexico.

"*Osewaninatta*," Mas couldn't help but to say, bowing his head. "Thanks so much." We Arais are in your debt.

"No, that's not necessary. Heard it all years ago. We did the best we could. Paid the property tax, but it was late one year. That was the year that the bank took it away from the Arais and sold the property to the highest bidder. Browning Gorman."

"Everbears," Mas murmured.

Miguel shook his head. "Same family, different generation. Clay Gorman's grandfather. He was the head of the bank, so he had an inside connection. We felt terrible but we did what we could. The Arais got themselves a lawyer. My father, even with his broken English, testified in court. The Arais were the early ones to come back to Watsonville, and in a matter of months, they got their house and greenhouses back."

Mas remembered talk of a lawyer and courts but never knew the whole story.

"You Japanese keep your feelings and thoughts to yourself, I know. Strong people. I went with my father to Salinas Fairgrounds right in the beginning, before they were shipped out to Arizona. I couldn't believe what I was seeing. This was a place for horses, but my classmates were there, sleeping and eating." Mas detected some moisture in Miguel's eyes. "All old man Arai wanted to talk about was those berries of his. The ones in his basement. He'd tell us to go down and plant them. So we did. Beautiful, beautiful sweet strawberries. I don't know what they crossed it with."

"What are you talkin' about?" Victor interrupted.

"Kids." Miguel threw up his arm as if he were ready to throw down some dice. "They know nothing about growing. Strawberries have a mother and father. Just like people. You take a berry with something special and pollinate with another berry with something special. That's why you call it 'birds and bees'—it's all about combining and making love."

Victor's face colored slightly. "Okay, I get the 'bee' part, but why do they say 'birds'?"

"I don't need to explain everything, do I? Anyway, these breeders act like the bees, spreading the pollen on the other thing on the strawberry plant."

Victor covered his ears. "I don't think that I want to hear this." He left for the front door.

"Going for his cigarette fix," Miguel said. "Terrible habit. Smoked two packs a day and see what happened to me. Triple bypass and my legs aren't worth a damn."

Mas was actually thankful to be alone with Miguel Duran, old man to old man. He had things he wanted to discuss, namely Jimi Jabami. "Whatchu think about Jabami?"

"Something happen to Jabami. Not sure exactly what. I think what happened to the Japanese just crushed him. And the mother. Oh, was she depressed. Lost the husband in that Arizona camp. I think it was tuberculosis. Now that was sad. Just think if he were over here. Maybe he wouldn't have died.

"Anyway, Jabami always had a chip on his shoulder about those strawberries that we planted for the Arais. Always claimed they were his."

Mas's ears perked up. This was the first for him to hear this.

"Oh, those strawberries, sweetest things you'd ever eat, I'm telling you. Sweet, sweet, sweet. But didn't last. Fragile. Just like a mistress."

Come to think of it, the Masao did taste pretty sweet, but as Billy confirmed, the meat didn't retain its firmness.

"We kept growing the crop, because I promised I would. And then Shug came back, so I gave him back every single strawberry plant. His father was crazy about the plants, too. But they didn't say anything to Jabami. I kept my mouth shut, too."

"Shug and his family owe you one, for sure. Oh, everytin' you did."

"Why do you think we're next door to each other? Not a coincidence. This was Arai land. Bought when Shug started making some real money."

Makes sense, Mas thought. The two families were now forever tied together.

"Minnie and Shug, they finally sold it to me in the sixties. Gave me a deal."

Mas had been wondering about a question from the beginning, but in no way could he ask the Arai family. But here, with an outsider with insider information, Mas found that he had the perfect opportunity. "What happen to the Stem House?"

"Well, if you didn't figure it out, Shug and Minnie's son

has an anger problem. Kind of like Shug, only Shug hid it better."

That was true, thought Mas. Shug's anger was buried deep, a sleeping dragon underneath the dunes. But if you poked the sand too much, the dragon, its mouth full of fire, would emerge.

"Shug and Billy were always at it. Kind of helped that Shug was doing all that traveling, moving around with his work. But Billy was still under him. One day, they were fighting—actually here, outside the house. My older son heard them. Billy yelling that Shug never let him grow and experiment, and Shug saying that Billy was a disgrace for leaving Sugarberry. I guess this was the time Billy told Shug he was moving on to Everbears. Because of everything that happened during the war, Shug was no fan of Everbears, or more specifically the Gorman family. I know you Japanese, you don't forget anything.

"So Billy takes off in his truck. Mad as hell, he was. I don't know where he was going. He didn't know himself, I think. So he was speeding right there on Beach Street—there was a car at a stop in front of him. He goes into the other lane and he didn't see it—a farmworker's kid on a bike with training wheels."

Mas felt numb. "Nobody say."

"I've never heard Shug or Minnie say anything of it. Billy was not arrested. It was accidental. The family was devastated, of course. The little girl had died by the time she got to the hospital.

"So the Arais decided to give the little girl's family the Stem House. Not a payoff, mind you. But just, I don't know, an apology, a symbol that Billy had done wrong."

Mas's head started pounding again, and it had nothing to do with the accident.

"It didn't end there, however. Through all the publicity, it was found out that the family of the little girl was not only undocumented, but the father was a wanted man. Had gotten in some trouble with the police some years back. So the father was deported back to Mexico and the wife followed." Miguel traced the margins of his sudoku grid with his pencil. "So the house still stands, the property of this deported Mexican family."

Is that why Billy had taken Mas on the midnight trip down memory lane? That for at least a few hours, he could recreate what the Stem House had meant to Shug and the rest of the gang?

"But nuttin' happening to house."

"Some folks—at least the farmworkers—think that's the punishment for what Billy did. That it stands there, ruined, so no one will ever forget."

All this disclosure was obviously taking a toll on Miguel. His speaking became slurred, and his eyes were starting to droop. Mas usually knew when he overstayed his welcome and that was probably a half hour ago.

"Come over again," Miguel told Mas as he headed for the front door. "It's always good to talk about old times."

Victor, the end of his cigarette glowing orange, was on the driveway washing the Impala. Soap suds made the pavement slippery, and Mas almost lost his footing.

"Hey, be careful," Victor admonished.

Mas took a few seconds to admire the boy's handiwork.

"Too bad about your wheels, man," Victor said. "The brakes just stopped working, huh? I heard that happens with old Ford trucks sometime."

Mas nodded. That is why he spent extra time checking the brakes before he left for Watsonville.

"You ever need to borrow one of our extra cars, just let us know."

The boy was obviously not offering his Impala, but the rickety, rusty Toyota and the trailer with two flat tires. It wasn't much of an offer, but Mas was still touched. He gave Victor a hand with drying the car's body.

"I'm actually thinking about selling this car."

"Oh, yah?" Mas was surprised. He knew firsthand how difficult it was to decide to abandon your vehicle for another.

"Thinking about going more professional, you know. Maybe a Lexus. BMW."

"Bizness must be good." Mas wrung the excess moisture out of his rag.

"Yeah, it's pretty good."

Mas never imagined that spying in farm country could afford a teenager a luxury car. Growing fruits and vegetables had definitely graduated to being a big business.

"Well, see ya." Before getting into his car, Victor exhaled a trail of smoke. Mas breathed in the nicotine remnants, remembering what it felt like when a young man thought he could conquer the world.

CHAPTER TEN

After resting for two days, Mas felt almost good as new. Mari said she was going to buy him a one-way airplane ticket from San Jose to Burbank. "The truck's gone, Dad," she said. "Forget about it and come home."

Mas did want to come home, but something was still nagging at him. Jimi Jabami. Miguel Duran had said that Jimi had a serious beef with the Arai family. Was it serious enough that Jimi would want to hurt Shug, just weeks before the announcement of the new strawberry?

Mas took a walk around the block, passing one-story ranch-style homes. Dogs wailed after him and at one house, he noticed that an inflatable bouncer was being set up in the back, most likely for a child's birthday later that day. When he arrived back at Minnie's, another car, a silver Honda, was parked in the driveway.

Mas turned the doorknob of the front door. It was unlocked, and when he entered, he heard voices in the living room.

It was a full house. He saw Alyssa Arai, the San Jose State student, sitting on the floor. Her brother was next to her in a chair. On the couch, Minnie sat next to Billy's wife, whose white roots showed in her otherwise neatly coifed hair.

Minnie smiled as Mas tentatively entered the living room. "Mas. You all know Mas. Colleen, you remember Mas Arai from Los Angeles, don't you? He was at the funeral."

Alyssa immediately lowered her head, so Mas knew she was embarrassed about what had transpired in her dorm. She must not have mentioned anything to the rest of her family. *I almost died because of you*, Mas thought, but whattheheck, he knew from experience that he shouldn't expect any gratitude from any young person. Her brother, dressed in a baseball uniform, looked up and grinned, while Colleen stayed frozen on the couch, her hands in her lap.

"Hallo," Mas said.

"Come join us," Minnie said, gesturing for Mas to sit down in Shug's old easy chair. "We're getting ready to go to Zac's game. He plays baseball for the community college up there in Aptos."

"Oh yah?" Mas said, sitting down.

"He starts, even though he's a first year."

"It's not that big of a deal, Grandma."

"You hit a double. Even I know that was good. What is your batting average now?"

"320."

"Your grandfather would have been so proud. He tried to make it to every home game."

Mas decided to take a chance and throw out a line. "So, you'zu the one who put the bat in Shug's coffin," he said to Zac.

Minnie frowned.

"Oh, that old bat from camp, right? I was talking to Aly about it. Like why it was in the coffin? Nobody put that in during the visitation. We thought you put it in there later, Grandma."

"It wasn't me. I left a photo and a note. I already told

Mas this." Her voice carried a hint of annoyance, a tone that everyone could detect.

"Maybe Dad?" Zac offered.

"Dad almost showed up late to the funeral, remember?" Alyssa crossed her arms.

"Maybe one of our aunties."

"Why would they put a bat in there?" Alyssa's usually smooth forehead was marred by anger lines. She turned to Mas. "Anyway, why do you care?"

"Alyssa," Colleen finally spoke, shocking the rest of them. Her voice was raspy but stern. "Don't be rude."

"No, I'm just wondering why he's bringing up the bat, Mom."

"I'm sorry," Colleen apologized to Mas.

Tears welled up in Alyssa's eyes. "I don't see why everything's my fault." She jumped up and ran toward the door.

"Alyssa!"

She was out the door; her mother could not stop her.

"I'll get her," said Zac, rising. "Maybe it's that time of the month or something."

Minnie pressed down on her slacks. "I think that we have time for some tea. Green tea, Colleen? *Ocha*, Mas?"

Mas shook his head vigorously, not wanting to be alone with Billy's wife.

"*Ocha* sounds good," said Colleen.

With Minnie disappearing into the kitchen, it was indeed just Mas with Colleen. They sat in silence for a good three minutes before Colleen began speaking. "The family's been under so much strain this past year. I'm afraid Billy and I haven't been very good parents."

Mas understood. His own parenting skills had been questionable, especially according to his daughter.

"I know what you did for Alyssa. Going to her dorm to warn her about the police coming over."

"Sheezu tell you?" Mas was surprised.

"She doesn't know that I know. Alyssa's ex-boyfriend came by the facility I was staying at and told me everything. Calling Laila was a prank. He eventually went to the police to confess."

Mas stayed quiet. Hearing "facility" made him feel scared. He knew that the "facility" wasn't home. Colleen must have been at the end of her rope, and Mas didn't know how long that rope was now.

"Billy made some mistakes. But I'm learning that I can't blame it all on him, even though I want to."

"Oh, well," Mas said. "Sometime can't control."

Colleen then surprised Mas by laughing. For a moment her voice sounded light and free. "You hit the nail on the head," she said. "Control. That's the struggle of my whole life."

The family piled into the silver Honda to go to Zac's game. Alyssa sat in the back, looking away from Mas.

Before they left, Minnie went up to Mas and gave him the keys to Shug's Lexus. "Feel free to get yourself some dinner. There's a nice Japanese restaurant on Beach that everyone goes to," she said. And then, more quietly, regarding Colleen: "She seems much better, doesn't she?"

Mas just grunted, because he didn't know how she was before.

"Even if they do divorce, she's still the mother of my grandchildren. She always will be." Minnie spoke definitively, as if she were trying to convince herself.

Mas didn't need any convincing. The silver Honda, transporting the college baseball star and his fans, went down the block and turned.

As he returned to the house, his stomach started to rumble. Japanese food would be good, he thought.

Mas drove Shug's Lexus to the Japanese restaurant. Its dashboard reminded him of an airplane pilot's cockpit with lit-up displays and controls. As he drove, he felt heat on his back. Damn. A warmer for the leather seats. Shug certainly did sit in the lap of luxury.

The Japanese restaurant had a small patch of green beside its parking lot—mostly bamboo and a grizzled pine that apparently had suffered its share of car exhaust. Inside, the small box of a room had mirrors on the walls and a mirrored disco ball hanging from the ceiling.

Mas's eyes were on the ball when he heard, "Hey, Mas."

Recognizing the voice, he felt a tinge of dread. Too late now.

Oily was at the sushi bar, and extended an arm to the empty seat beside him. "Come join me."

Mas wasn't sure if Oily was there to eat. He was certainly there to drink, judging from the empty glasses in front of him. One still had some liquid, along with something gray floating in it.

"Whatsu dat?"

"Oyster shooters. You know, umm, *kaki.*"

"Yah, I knowsu *kaki.* Gotsu plenty in Hiroshima."

"I'll get you one."

"No, no condition. My *atama.*" Mas pointed to his banged-up head.

"Concussion, right? Had a dozen of those when I was playing football. Drinking is the best antidote to concussions, my friend." Oily was never good at listening, and he obviously wasn't going to start now. "Doi-*san,* an oyster shooter for my friend," Oily ordered from the owner, who doubled as the bartender and cashier.

"*Hai.*"

The oyster shooter came, and Mas had to agree, it went down smoothly. A cool tang and snap. He thought he might be in love. Another oyster shooter and then warm sake, smooth again with a comforting burn at the roof of his mouth. Oily was right. Mas was starting to feel better. Next came sake on the rocks, cool and refreshing, a *suppai* taste in the middle of his tongue that made his insides contract.

Mas's head started to swim with all the liquor. The disco ball seemed to be moving—in fact, the whole room had become a blur of faces and voices.

The alcohol hadn't slowed Oily down. In fact, it seemed to have opened him up. He started talking about each of his ex-wives, each woman's merits and weaknesses. Then he moved onto work. How he was depending on Billy to introduce a strong, one-of-a-kind varietal in a season of strawberry yellows.

"I told him that the strawberry had to be clean. Clean all

the way to the mothers," Oily said. "Guess what he's calling his berry?"

Mas had no idea.

"Shigeo. You know, in memory of Shug."

Mas had been so used to calling Shug by his nickname that he'd forgotten that his friend had a proper Japanese first name.

"So, any leads on what Shug and Linus are introducing?"

Oily obviously thought he could take advantage of Mas's inebriation. "Shug dead," Mas slurred.

"But that doesn't mean the varieties are dead. He'd been working with Linus this whole time."

Linus, the name sounded familiar.

"You know, Linus Verdorben. The other hybridizer over at Everbears."

The giant elf who had been at Minnie's house. "Yah, yah," Mas said. "I knowsu him."

"They'd been working on it over at Linus's house in Castroville."

Castroville? No one had mentioned Castroville, the king of the artichoke.

Oily grinned proudly, his wide smile making him look like a jack o'lantern. "I followed Shug one day. Followed him over to Linus's. He lives in some trailers next to his old man's gas station. He's got an artichoke painted on one side of a trailer."

"Huh?" Mas thought he might have heard Oily wrong. Hell, with all this alcohol, he certainly could have.

"That Linus is a *sukebe,* and a real one, I'm telling you."

Mas, his face bright red, chuckled. To hear Oily call

another man a *sukebe* meant the other guy was quite a pervert.

"He walks around his lab with no clothes on."

Mas raised his eyebrows.

"I'm not kiddin', *yo*. Shug even told me. Linus says his creative juices work better when he feels free."

"Shug jokin'. Shug wouldn't hang around nobody like dat."

Oily's chin jutted out. "Typical, Mas. You putting Shug on some pedestal. You were always by his side. Defending him. I know what you did for Shug."

"*Nanda?*" Mas asked in Japanese. *What?*

"You know, the time you took the hit for Shug. Back in Salinas. Why did you do it?"

On that early summer day, it was thirst that drove Mas and Shug to search for a liquor store. They were in Salinas and it was 1949. They had just delivered crates of late strawberries from Jabami Farms, and they wanted to be rewarded for their efforts.

Salinas wasn't that far from Watsonville, only thirty miles south. But it was a different world. The coastal air somehow softened Watsonville, like opaque curtains waffling in a ocean-scented breeze. Salinas, on the other hand, was a harsh, real agricultural town. It was big, much bigger than Watsonville, with more history and more anger.

Mas and Shug were dusty and dirty. But they wanted a drink, and they couldn't find a liquor store.

So they went into a bar. It was named after some kind

of reptile that Mas couldn't pronounce. To clearly make its point, a bronze lizard, its long tongue protruding, perched on a pedestal near the door. Shug and Mas made their way to the wooden bar.

"Two beers, please," Shug said.

"You got it," the bartender, his back turned, said. He began filling two glasses with beer and then swung around. His face fell and grew hard. The beers remained in his hands.

Mas suddenly noticed all the military memorabilia surrounding them. An American flag hung on one side of the wall. There was a Veterans of Foreign Wars plaque, with a framed newspaper article on the return of Salinas-born soldiers who had survived the Bataan death march in the Philippines.

"What are you, Japs?" the bartender asked. A few other men at the bar turned, their faces bearing the same grim expressions.

"No, sir," Shug said in his best college-boy voice. "We are Japanese Americans. Born here in the U.S. of A. We are not Japs."

The bartender wiped his hands on his apron. "He looks like a Jap. Let me hear him speak."

Mas felt sweat pour down his hairline. He pushed Shug. "Letsu go," he mumbled.

"No, sir," said Shug. "He's not your paid monkey. He's a person and he's not going to say something just because you want him to." What was Shug doing? This was not the time to fight.

"Well, then, the two of you can get the hell out of my bar."

"Letsu go." Mas jerked hard at Shug's arm. He still wouldn't move, so Mas thought he'd lead the way. Good riddance, he thought, crossing through the doorway back outside. Why be somewhere you are not wanted?

"Mas, Mas," Shug jogged toward him.

Mas stopped and waited.

"Look what I have." Shug opened up his jacket to reveal the bronze lizard, its mouth wide open.

"Shug!"

"Hey, you!" The bartender was in the doorway, his finger pointing right at Shug.

Shug dropped the lizard and ran. Mas followed, his workboots digging into the sand and spraying gravel all around him.

He felt something pull at his shirt. Run, run. *Hashire. Hashire.* Then a tackling of his legs, and Mas fell flat on his face, grains of sand stinging his cheeks and eyes.

"You goddamn Jap thief," said the bartender, his chest heaving from running so hard. "We've already called the cops."

"Wait!" Shug had stopped, but Mas waved him away.

"No, I take it," Mas said. "I steal."

"I'll get help," Shug said before running off to the truck.

The bartender held onto Mas's arm, pulling it so hard that Mas feared it would be torn from its socket. He made Mas sit on the ground outside the bar, right next to a spot where someone had vomited recently.

Mas wasn't scared, however. He'd gotten into trouble before in Hiroshima. So when the policeman came in his black-and-white Ford, he showed no emotion.

"He bloody admitted it to me," the bartender claimed, but now, since Shug was gone, Mas saw no reason to make a false confession. He stayed quiet.

The officer put him in the back seat and drove him to the Monterey County Jail. There he was photographed, fingerprinted, and searched. He was finally led to a large holding cell filled with scrawny white boys. There were also a few dark, short men like Mas. Only they spoke Spanish, so they were most likely *braceros*, the temporary workers brought from Mexico.

A couple of men spat "Jap" toward Mas, but he didn't care. It was strange: Inside the jail, slurs seemed a rite of passage, but on the outside, they had much more bite.

He spent only one night in jail. The next morning, they called out his name, and he figured that Shug had come to his rescue and posted bail. But in the waiting area was someone he didn't expect. Ats, wearing a sweater over a cotton dress.

"Jimi gave me the money," she said. Jimi also provided for an attorney, who was able to immediately dismiss the charges. Mas ended up paying Jimi back in free labor.

Shug apologized countless times for putting Mas in that position, but Mas waved him off. "No *shinpai*." What was one night in a jail cell? He had experienced far, far worse.

But if he really admitted it to himself, he did feel somewhat branded now in Watsonville. The town knew he'd been taken into police custody, and of course no one bothered to get the facts.

"So why did you do it?" Oily repeated.

Shug, unlike Mas, was destined for better things. He was a college boy at UC Davis. Mas, on the other hand, was basically a migrant farm worker. If they could go back in time, Mas would have done the same thing all over again.

Mas didn't answer Oily. Instead he said, "Mo' sake."

Oily let out a low whistle. "So that's why."

"Huh?"

"Now I get it. That's why Shug named his new variety Masao."

Was that the reason? thought Mas. Was his insistence on taking the blame for Shug's theft of the bronze lizard reason enough to be immortalized in a newfangled berry?

The restaurant owner refused to serve them any more drinks until they got food in their stomachs. So it was one *nigiri* after the other, and miso soup, and *chawan mushi*, a delectable egg custard cooked with shrimp and shiitake mushrooms. Plus cup of tea after cup of tea. Soon the doors were closing, and both Mas and Oily had forgotten about their oyster shooters.

"You okay driving, Mas?" Oily asked in the parking lot.

Mas nodded. Oily apparently lived close enough to walk home.

I'll just take a quick nap, Mas told himself. Just a little pick-me-up before the drive back to Minnie's.

CHAPTER ELEVEN

A knock, getting louder and faster.

The light, even diffused by the fog, blinded Mas. He squinted his eyes toward something moving through the frosted windows. Wiping the misted surface with the side of his arm, he could clearly see Minnie, the front of her hair in rollers.

When he opened the car door, the cold air poured into the Lexus and soaked into his bones.

"Mas, you scared the daylights out of me. When I woke up and you still weren't back, I thought something had happened to you."

"Just took a little *hirune*. What time?"

"That was some nap, Mas. It's five o'clock in the morning."

Mas's head pounded, and he didn't think that it was the concussion. It was that *bakatare* Oily's oyster shooters, not to mention sake cup after sake cup.

"Here, let me drive us home." Minnie helped Mas out of the driver's seat into the passenger side. She was going to leave her car in the parking lot and pick it up later.

She crinkled her nose. "You were drinking."

"Dinner with Oily."

"So you were definitely drinking. Drinking alcohol with a concussion. Not such a good idea."

Mas rubbed the stubble over his lip and on his chin.

That's what he'd told Oily. Too bad he didn't listen to his own advice.

"You'll see him again in a few hours," Minnie said. "He and Evelyn are coming by to help Billy and me with the last of the thank-yous for the *koden*."

Funeral work never seemed to be finished. Mas recalled his thank-you notes taking weeks upon weeks to get out. Actually, to be perfectly honest, he didn't write one thank-you; it had all been his daughter Mari's doing.

"I'll let you rest for a while," Minnie said as she parked Shug's car in the garage. "Hope we don't make too much noise."

His head still banging, Mas pressed down on his temples.

As he pulled on the door handle, he saw something on the otherwise immaculate floor on the passenger side. Shug wasn't the type to leave even a single dust speck on the interior of his car, so out of respect, Mas picked up the piece of paper, a receipt, and stuck it his sweatshirt pocket.

The calls from creditors were getting more frequent, frequent enough for Jimi to pull out the telephone cord from its wall outlet. He didn't answer his cell phone anymore unless the calls came from his children, employees, or suppliers. He didn't bother to listen to his voicemail messages; almost every single one of them seemed to be from collection agencies.

And then came the letter. The foreclosure notice from their bank informing Jimi that he needed to settle up the delinquent mortgage payments within thirty days. Six months' worth of principal, interest, and other additional costs. If he failed to this, not only the house but the farm would be subject to foreclosure.

The letter was a sign, and its timing was also a sign. Ats's caretaker would be off for the weekend. She'd packed her overnight bag, apparently a free duffel from a casino in Laughlin, and told Jimi that she was excited to see her sister, who was visiting from the Philippines. Jimi told her to enjoy herself and take an extra day if she needed to.

Watching the caretaker leave in a relative's car, Jimi didn't waste any time. He retrieved the package from their extra refrigerator in the packing shed. The pills inside looked innocuous, like aspirin. He ground the extra-strong morphine in a mortar until it was a fine white dust. Then mixed it with apple juice. It was only a matter of Ats drinking it. But she wasn't having one drop.

"Ats," he said, hoping that evoking her name would elicit a better response. She continued to stare at him plaintively with her large eyes, her eyelashes now few and far between, like a flower losing its petals. She knew. But how?

Her lips were tight against her closed teeth.

We are going to lose the farm, Jimi thought. *We are going to lose my parents' legacy.* He felt defeated. This was all for the next generation. Their children and grandchildren. What did his and Ats's lives mean anyway? It had to mean more than providing strawberries on top of someone's shortcake or pie. It needed to have more substance. Something tangible. Dirt and ground. Something that could be fertilized and irrigated. A variety named Taro would have been special. Even if nobody else knew, the Jabamis would know that strawberry was theirs. Well, perhaps the Arais have won, Jimi thought. He wiped away tears from the corners of his eyes.

Abandoning the fatal morphine and apple juice concoction on the kitchen table, he went outside. He sat underneath the lemon trees and spoke to his sisters. *At least I tried.*

"Mas, it's for you. A woman named Genessee."

Minnie had opened the guest bedroom door, and Mas blinked his eyes awake. What time was it? He took the cordless phone from Minnie, who took her time leaving the room.

Mas sat up on the bed. "Hallo."

"I'm so sorry to call you at your cousin's house. I hadn't heard from you and I was worried."

"I'zu *orai*. Comin' along good."

"I'm so relieved. Mari said you told them not to come. Just making sure that you weren't being Japanese."

Mas was confused. Well, he was Japanese, in a manner of speaking. Although he was officially American, it was hard to erase his cultural DNA.

He talked to Genessee a little more, although he didn't go into the details of the whole mess swirling around the Arai household. It was too hard to make out anything definitive; every time he tried to grasp hold of something, it moved, only to be replaced with something else in flight. As always, though, it grounded Mas to talk to Genessee. The rest of them in the house must have noticed, because when he went out to the living room to replace the phone in its cradle, everyone was giving him a funny look.

"So, was that your giiiirlfriend, Mas?" Evelyn's voice took on a terrible sing-song tone that made Mas cringe.

"Just like you to keep someone under wraps. So who is she?" Mas couldn't believe that Oily could bounce back so strong after a hard night of drinking. Oily lifted a glass filled with liquid. He couldn't be starting again so early in the day, could he?

"Well, her first name is Genessee. Unusual. Related to anyone we would know?" Minnie asked.

Mas feared it was a losing battle. "No, no."

"Is she a *hakujin* woman?" Minnie wasn't going to let up.

"Uhnnn," Mas said, hedging again. "*Hapa*. Part Okinawan."

"*Hapa* makes her half-white."

"Uhnnn," Mas repeated. *Oh, what the hell, need to come clean.* "Sheezu *kokujin*."

"Wow, that's very Los Angeles of you." Mas didn't know if Oily was paying him a compliment or insulting him. When it came to Oily, there was always a sarcastic twist, so Mas assumed he meant a little of both.

"A *kurochan*," Evelyn murmured, without thinking.

Mas blanched. He himself had used that slur in the past, but he didn't approve of it now, especially to describe his lady friend.

"I don't know much Japanese, but isn't that derogatory?" Billy, who must have been lying on the couch this whole time, got up.

"Billy, there's no one here to hear it," Minnie said.

"You mean it would be all right for a bunch of black

people to call us Japs behind our backs?"

"It's not the same," Minnie said.

"It sounds pretty much the same to me."

"Billy, stop it."

Billy shook his head. "I have to go. I have to take care of some things for Laila." He put on his tennis shoes and left out the front door.

Minnie addressed the people in her living room as if she were issuing a public apology. "I'm sorry, everyone. It's that Laila. It's almost like he misses her more than his own father." She tightened her fists and pressed them into her eyes. More waterworks.

Evelyn immediately went to her friend's side, while Oily continued to sip his "juice."

Mas chose to go outside to follow Shug's son, who hadn't quite made it back into his truck.

"I just get tired of it sometimes, you know," he said to Mas in the driveway.

Mas, surprisingly, did know. Two large boxes sat in the bed of Billy's truck. "Where'su you goin'?"

"Laila's parents' house. I have to go over there now. Drop off some of Laila's things. Some old photos that she brought to the apartment. Some clothing. I was going to just mail them over, but I figure that would be a chickenshit thing to do. I need to see them face to face."

It was a no-brainer for Mas, who didn't relish dealing with all the nosy ones back in the house. "I'zu goin' wiz you."

At first, the ride was dead quiet, but as they got on the highway and the scenery got more uncontrolled and even wild— the wind-swept cypress frozen in a dervish dance—Billy's lips got looser. It was as if getting away from Watsonville, even only a few miles, made him more relaxed and reflective. "My whole life, I've tried to follow the rules," he said, sunglasses shading his eyes. "Do what my parents want me to do. Get married, have kids. Get involved in the business of making strawberries. Then I took a good long look at what I had. What? Colleen and I met in college. I didn't know who I was and neither did she. We got together because everyone expected us to."

Another cypress, this one shaped like a man running in place.

"You know, Everbears wanted to send me to Mexico. This was after something had happened here. Something real bad. I needed to get away. They wanted me to try breeding some plants down there. New climate, new soil. A new start. But Colleen said absolutely not. She said she was afraid of being shot, killed. That's just TV shows, I told her. Sensational news programs."

Billy sipped something from a metal thermos in the cup holder in between the seats. "And then I met Laila at a pool party thrown by Clay. They went to high school together. We fought like cats and dogs from the get-go. Later we were both manning booths at the local farmers' market—I was supposed to teach people about breeding strawberries, and she was there to tell us how laboratories had no place in creating organic fruit. We went out for drinks to continue to debate; one thing led to another, and we were in love."

Mas had to stop himself from snorting. Love. Young people always were concerned with love. Why didn't they have the good sense that he and Genessee seemed to have? Restraint.

"I didn't hide anything from Colleen," Billy explained. "That wouldn't be right to her and it wouldn't be right to Laila. I told Colleen that she could keep the house. I'd pay for college for the kids. I'd give her alimony, too. I wouldn't fight her for anything." Billy readjusted his sunglasses. "I didn't expect her to shut down. I guess she had dreams, too. That we would get old together, play with our grandchildren. That was her dream, my nightmare. There was no compromise."

He turned after getting off the highway. The skies were gray, but Mas lowered the passenger-side window and let the cool air bathe his face. He always felt transformed in Monterey. He didn't feel like he was in California or even in the United States. It was like he'd been transported to a magical world where there was no poverty, no crime. For a moment, he felt happy. Then he was brought back to reality by Billy's continuing talk.

"So you have your Genessee. And I had my Laila. I don't regret anything. Just that she's gone."

They passed the immaculate golf course that bordered the cliffs by the sea, and then turned onto a narrow, windy street lined with estates that each stretched about a block in size. The young maid, Cecilia, had mentioned that Laila came from a wealthy family, but Mas didn't imagine this kind of opulent environment.

"Her parents didn't let me say goodbye to her. I'll never forgive them for that. They never approved of me. I mean, I

can't say that I blame them. I'm still officially married, with
kids only ten years younger than Laila."

Billy slowed the truck and stopped in front of a huge
Mediterranean-style mansion that reminded Mas of ones he
had seen in Glendale, California.

"That's where she grew up."

Behind the tall wrought-iron fencing, Mas saw a rolling
lawn that alone seemed to span at least a quarter of an acre.
There was a grove of pine and cypress trees to one side and a
large stone fountain in the middle of the property. This was
not a one-gardener job, but a multiple-gardener one. And
odds are they came here many times a week.

Billy stopped at the black gate in front of the driveway
and pressed the intercom button. "I'm here with Laila's
things," he said, and the gate slowly opened to a neat cobble-
stone driveway. Before they even parked in the driveway that
circled the fountain, a woman appeared at the door.

She was blonde like her daughter, but her face was completely different. Mas had seen photos of the live Laila, and
she'd had a thin nose and bright blue eyes. The mother's face
was broad with a strong chin, and her dark brown eyes sim-
mered with emotion. Right now the emotional dial seemed
to be turned to hate, or at least strong dislike.

Without expressing any greeting, she quickly accepted
the box from Billy.

"I want you to know that I didn't hurt her. I would have
never hurt her," Billy said. He just couldn't keep his mouth
shut.

The brown eyes burned. "You can say whatever you
want. We don't believe a single word."

Billy muttered something under his breath. "Well, you have her stuff now," he said and headed back to the truck, leaving Mas with the second box. Mas didn't know what to do. Leave the box in the middle of the driveway? However uncomfortable he was, he was going to be a gentleman, at least when it came to hauling boxes. "I carry for youzu," he said.

Mrs. Smith first hesitated but with her own hands full, relented. "Here, follow me."

Going in the house, Mas attempted to take off his shoes, but she said it was not necessary. "You can put it down here," she said, referring to a low coffee table in what seemed like the living room. The floors were marble; he felt like he was inside a mausoleum. He set down the box and turned to leave, but the woman called him back, asking, "Who are you, anyway?"

"Billy's relative. I'zu Arai, too. Come for Shug's funeral."

"Yes, yes, Laila told us about that. I am sorry for your loss."

Mas held his arms awkwardly at his sides. He almost felt that he need to be officially dismissed.

"How long have you known Billy?"

"Ever since heezu boy," Mas said. That was true enough.

"Everyone we met in Watsonville says he didn't do it. That he's not capable of such violence. But we know now that he killed that little girl on the bicycle."

"Dat accident."

"Well, that might be. But the Watsonville police don't have any other suspects in Laila's death. They don't even have the murder weapon; that's how ridiculous this whole investigation is. We're bringing in our own private detective. A detective who will get to the bottom of this."

"Good for youzu," Mas said, and he meant it. He understood that the mention of the detective was his signal to leave. Crossing over the marble rotunda, he noticed a photo collage on an easel by the door. "Laila," the lettering read, followed by a drawing of a yellow Hawaiian flower. Dozens of photos from Laila's past had been cut and pasted together.

"That was from the funeral service," Mrs. Smith said.

Mas stopped to take a look. Laila, her hair almost white as a child, looked so happy, effervescent. As she grew into her teenage years, she had none of the gawkiness that Mari had. In the photos, she was lean but well proportioned, with beautiful blonde hair down to her waist.

He noticed a more formal photo, Laila in a long lavender dress next to a skinny boy who resembled a wet dog in a tuxedo. *Ara*—Mas had seen that face before. Billy's boss at Everbears. What was his name again?

Mrs. Smith noticed Mas's interest in her daugher's date.

"You know Clay Gorman, the CEO of Everbears? He was Laila's high-school sweetheart. It was Clay who got Laila interested in strawberries in the first place."

"I told you Laila wouldn't want that photo up there," a high-pitched voice called from the living room. It came from a surprising figure, an exact mini-version of Laila, with the same long golden hair.

"Clay was part of her life, an important part. And look how much he's been offering to help with everything."

"They weren't friends, Mom. Not at the end." The young woman, not even bothering to acknowledge Mas, marched up to the display and tore the photo of the young couple from the collage.

"Kekai!" Mrs. Smith chided her daughter, but she'd disappeared from the rotunda. Seemingly embarrassed, Mrs. Smith attempted a smile and shrugged her shoulders. "Daughters," she said.

"What took you so long?" Billy asked when Mas finally returned to the truck.

"Laila gotsu lil sister?"

"Oh, she was the 'surprise' child. Kekai is still in college. Goes to UC Santa Cruz. She was home?"

Mas nodded.

"I got a chance to meet her a couple of times. Laila was always protective of her. She thought her sister was too naïve about the world." Billy became quiet for a moment. "But seeing what happened to Laila," he finally continued, "It might have been Laila who was too naïve."

It was way past dinnertime when Billy finally dropped Mas off. "Thanks for coming with me," he said. "It actually was good not to do that by myself."

Mas grunted and raised the back of his hand as a goodbye as he made his way to the front door. He used Minnie's extra key to get into the house, which was empty. A note was waiting for him on the kitchen counter: Minnie's friend had invited her to the movies, and she'd be coming home late. Next to the note was a ham sandwich, but after the night of drinking, Mas still didn't have the stomach for food. *Mah*, he thought, *Oily did me in good this time.*

He stuffed his hands in his sweatshirt pockets and his left hand came up with a bit of paper, the receipt from Shug's car floor. Mas retrieved his reading glasses. It was for a fried artichoke from somewhere in Castroville. He checked the date. Two weeks ago. Mas went to Minnie's calendar, obviously a freebie from a Japanese market in San Jose. He traced the day. It was the day before Shug was found dead in his home. What had Minnie said, that Shug had a bout of stomach flu before he died? Then why was he eating a fried artichoke? Unless it had been the artichoke that gave him food poisoning.

Oily had mentioned Castroville, Mas remembered from the fog of last night. Castroville was where that scientist, Linus Verdorben, had his laboratory. Hadn't Billy mentioned that Laila had gone to Castroville to steal one of the Masao plants?

Mas pressed his forehead with his hands, as if to put his broken *atama* together again. He would need the little he had to deal with a genius hybridizer.

It was not difficult to find Linus Verdorben's residence. First of all, Castroville was not a large town, maybe five thousand people. The whole area, shaped like a sock, could be contained in maybe one square mile. Even though it had been literally decades since Mas had wandered through the artichoke town, he knew his gas stations, which tended to stay put. Verdorben's was not open for business, but the old gas pumps hadn't gone anywhere. They stood like double headstones underneath a metal awning. And sure enough, an image of an artichoke, cut in half, was painted on the side of a trailer next to the pumps.

Mas steered the Lexus onto the dirt driveway. A barbed-wire fence protected beds of strawberries in the back. Mas didn't know why, but he felt on edge. Maybe even slightly afraid.

After getting out of the car, he went to the trailer and rapped his knuckles on the flimsy door. In a matter of seconds, the door flew open.

"Masao Arai," Linus said, as if he were expecting him. "So happy you are here."

Linus was not fully naked, but he was not fully dressed either. Bare-chested, he wore a Hawaiian-print sarong around his waist. His skin was pasty, the shade of flour, and his stomach protruded proudly over his cotton wrap.

"Come in, come in."

Welcoming Mas on the facing wall was a giant rose in full bloom. Painted in the same style as the artichoke mural, the rose petals were completely open, revealing thick yellow anthers balanced on skinny stamens. There was something human, even *sukebe* about the image.

"That's a rose from my garden. I like to take pictures, as well as draw them."

Inside, the trailer looked nothing like the outside. It was plush, with a hardwood floor and velvet furniture. Linus extended his hand toward a velvet chair shaped like giant lips. Mas declined his offer.

"So, Masao, such a pleasure, such a pleasure. How are you finding your stay in Watsonville?"

What a strange thing to be saying, Mas thought. It wasn't like he was on a pleasure vacation. Actually nosing around in Arai business was hard work, maybe even harder than gardening.

"Now, I've heard that you are a survivor of the blast in Hiroshima. How amazing that is. Unbelievable. Now, how close were you to the hypocenter?"

Mas was doubly shocked. This was only the second time he'd laid eyes on Linus, and the scientist was asking him personal questions about his past?

Linus must have sensed that he had offended Mas. "Let's start over," he said. "How can I help you?"

"Shug in Castroville. Day he die." Mas removed the receipt for the fried artichokes from his wallet.

"Oh, yes. Well, we're not quite sure when he died, are we? But yes, Shug stopped by here after picking up those artichokes. He wasn't feeling very well, that's for sure. He loves those fried artichokes, but he couldn't eat them that day. His stomach was bothering him." Linus adjusted the sarong around his waist. Mas was afraid he might loosen the knot rather than tighten it. "What I would do is check on what he ate earlier that day. I would actually pay a visit to Jimi Jabami."

"Jimi Jabami?" Mas asked.

"Shug told me that Jimi came by out of the blue to give him a pie."

CHAPTER TWELVE

By the time Mas got back to Minnie's house, the neighborhood was pitch black. There weren't too many streetlights to begin with, and the ones that were there happened to be dim.

The porch light was on, however, and when Mas pushed open the door, the dining room was lit, with papers spread all over the table. Dressed in her pajamas and robe, Minnie sat with a pen in her hand. She looked at Mas from above her reading glasses.

"Mas, please sit down. Evelyn's going to tell you herself, but she's very sorry. She didn't mean to say anything insulting. We're still a little *inaka* over here. I mean, we're changing like the rest of the world, but sometimes our words don't reflect it."

"No *shinpai*," Mas said, sitting down. He had forgotten all about Evelyn's rude comment.

"Where were you?"

"Castro-bi-ru. Montcrcy."

"You saw Linus."

Mas nodded.

"And—" Minnie waited.

"Dunno. Shug was goin' ova there eberyday."

"To develop their strawberry."

Mas nodded again.

"That figures. That's no surprise, I guess. But why was Shug making it such a secret?" Minnie removed her reading glasses from the bridge of her nose. "And Monterey. You and Billy went to Laila's parents' house."

Mas drummed his fingers on the table.

"I heard they live in a mansion there. Own houses in San Jose, Kona, and even Hong Kong. To tell you the truth, I didn't know what Laila was doing with Billy."

Mas wasn't sure himself. "Gettin' a detective," he told Minnie. A real one.

"To find Laila's killer? That's good. I'm glad they are."

Mas carefully watched Minnie's eyes. Was she really glad?

She quickly changed the subject, waving her hands over her paperwork.

"So much to do still, even after the funeral. Did you change over all your bank accounts right away?"

Mas was embarrassed that Mari had handled most of his financial matters after Chizuko passed away. *Yakunitatanai*, you don't have much usefulness, Chizuko would have said to him at the time.

"I have to wait at least another two weeks for the death certificate, I guess."

Mas realized that there was some organization in Minnie's piles of paper. Next to the bank accounts, he saw a document with the letterhead of the Santa Cruz County Coroner's Office.

"Whatsu dis?" Mas couldn't help but ask.

"Oh, the coroner's report. The one they issued a few days after the autopsy. Just basic things. Contents in stomach, that type of thing."

Without even asking permission, Mas began reading the report.

"He had some kind of stomach flu before he died, so there wasn't much in there."

"Strawberry," Mas murmured.

"Isn't that something? So ironic. The last thing he ate was strawberries."

But that wasn't the only thing. The other thing, according to the report, was rhubarb.

The first and last time Mas tried rhubarb was in Watsonville.

Jabami Farms always had some rows of field rhubarb, the green, full leaves hiding the long, popsicle-pink stalks. Mas had never heard of rhubarb before, but Oily and Shug would often get into debates about whether it was a vegetable or fruit.

Ats decided that she would bake a strawberry rhubarb pie. It would be a surprise for the crew, and more importantly, a surprise for Jimi.

After taking a small bite, Mas couldn't help but pucker his face. *Suppai!*

"Does it taste all right? A little too tart, huh?" Ats asked.

The boys just kept quiet, but leave it to Evelyn to deliver the truth without any diplomacy. "Golly, Ats, it's as sour as sour can be!"

Ats blinked away her tears, and Mas made up his mind to eat every single bite. He lived to regret it, however, because everyone who ate the pie got sick.

They took turns running to the toilet at the Stem House.

"Oh my gosh, what have I done?" wailed Ats, her face flushed.

They found out soon enough when they next convened at Jabami Farms. Jimi Jabami, stone-faced, stood in the middle of the rhubarb plants. "You could have killed somebody," he scolded Ats. "You never eat the leaves. They are poisonous. You just use the stalks."

"Oh." Ats's lips actually formed the shape of an "O." She was terribly embarrassed, but she didn't make a mad dash through the fields to escape her shame. Instead she stood squarely in front of them in her pedal pushers and sneakers. "I'm so sorry, everyone."

"Hey, we're alive," Oily joked.

"No *shinpai*," said Mas, telling her not to worry.

"Thank God I didn't eat much," commented Evelyn.

From that point on, Mas vowed never to eat rhubarb again. Sure, there were people in Japan who didn't mind spending thousands of yen on a poisonous blowfish, but he figured that was for those who never really stared death square in the face. Mas, on the hand, had seen death too many times, and he wasn't about to willingly invite it into his life.

Over the years, Jimi Jabami must have experimented with rhubarb, just because he was that type of man. Mas had heard that his father, Goro, had been the same. Goro and Wataru Arai, actually, were cut from the same kind of cloth—Issei men who were pioneers, inquisitive. They were unafraid.

Mas could visualize Jimi in front of his stove, boiling down vats of rhubarb leaves. Perhaps he first tested his deadly concoction on rodents, mice. Maybe even snakes. Was Shug his first human victim? Or had there been more?

It had been so easy, thought Jimi. So easy. But he knew that from being a cook all his life. Once you appeared with any kind of baked good—apple pie, German chocolate cake, oatmeal-raisin cookies—most people stopped thinking. They only responded with their eyes and stomachs. And Shug Arai was no different.

He hadn't been eating well, he told Jimi, since Minnie had left town a week earlier.

"It's a bit early for the rhubarb," Jimi responded. "Someone at the temple mentioned that you were on your own, so I thought I'd bring this by."

Shug looked confused at first, and then strangely touched. Jimi hadn't been friendly like this in years, maybe decades. What had Shug been thinking? Perhaps that Ats's sickness had softened Jimi?

Jimi thought it was all hubris. Shug's pride that people would be talking about him, worried about him.

Jimi handed off the mini-pie, a perfect single serving for a gluttonous man. The crust had turned out perfectly, a glossy golden.

"Would you like to come in?" Shug asked.

No, no. He had to get back to Ats. Jimi bowed his head slightly and took his time going down Shug's porch steps. As soon as he heard the screen door and then the regular door close behind him, he smiled. The big shot would eat his poison, and there wouldn't be anyone to save him.

Jimi spent the morning in his rhubarb fields. Harvesting rhubarb was easy, just twisting the stalk and tearing it off. He loved to hear the snap, just like fresh celery stalks make. Today he had a knife to remove the fan-shaped killer leaves on the other end.

It felt therapeutic, as if he was actually accomplishing something. The caregiver was back from her trip and inside with Ats, so he had a few hours to himself.

In the distance, he saw a car parked on the side of the road, near his mailbox. Wasn't that Shug's car? Jimi dropped his knife. And was that Shug coming toward him?

Jimi cupped his eyes and then relaxed. It was Mas Arai, the man with nine lives. He used one of them up in Hiroshima, then another when his truck crashed on Hecker Pass. How many other times had he survived danger? How many more lives did the old man still have left?

Mas didn't bother with saying "hallo." He'd come for business. Purely business. When Jimi saw the hard line of Mas's mouth, he understood. He picked up his knife.

"*Hayai, ne*, for rhubarb," Mas said.

"Yup. Early. Came out of nowhere." Snap, snap.

"No rhubarb in Japan," Mas said. At least not in Hiroshima.

"There is something that tastes a little like it. Knotweed. Part of it looks like bamboo."

Mas nodded. He was familiar with that. *Itadori.* "*Itadori* leaves like rhubarb. Poison." Back in Hiroshima, their garden had its share of *itadori*. A stray cat had wandered into their yard one day; the next day, it was found dead hiding underneath the shade of some maple trees. *Itadori* was the culprit, insisted Mas's mother, a cat lover. The *itadori* was pulled out immediately.

Rhubarb leaves fell off the stalk with one movement of Jimi's knife. The fields were so quiet now. A breeze moved through the ranch, and Mas swore he could hear the leaves rubbing again each other.

Jimi stood up from his work. "What do you want?"

"Shug neva do nuttin' against you. Not really." Mas still didn't understand why Jimi would want to take his second cousin's life.

Jimi frowned. He wasn't sure how to react. Was this a trap? It well could be.

"Those strawberries, *mukashi no hanashi.*"

Jimi felt anger rise to his head. He knew what this Arai was trying to do. Throw in some Japanese words in an attempt to disarm or maybe even charm him. But *just things of the past*? Really? Was he supposed to forgive and forget? Oh, no, it was not that simple.

"You're not from here. You don't know."

"I born here."

"Watsonville may be on your birth certificate, but you don't know what it feels like to get a notice that you need to leave your life for a shitty fairground with thousands of other people. To get the runs and stand in line for the bathroom with no stalls. To leave a field of ripe strawberries, the best crop you've ever had, for birds to eat. To watch your daddy die in the desert from all that dust. You don't know jack shit."

Mas couldn't debate Jimi. The old man was right. Mas didn't know. But Shug, Minnie, and the rest did. Why so much hate toward them?

"And then I see Shug Arai, riding so high. UC Davis grad, some kind of genius. And our strawberries—our strawberry variety—being stolen from us. What the hell did he think he was doing? Going to save the day with his strawberry? Make his millions with his strawberry?

"Then I heard what they're calling it. The Masao. Your name. Why? You had nothing to do with that strawberry. So why you?"

Mas, ironically, had to agree.

"So Shug gets rich. But what about the rest of us?" Jimi's head began to shake.

"So you goes ova there with a pie. Rhubarb pie."

"Can't prove anything. So what if one of the last things Shug ate was the pie? Doesn't mean a thing."

Mas turned and starting walking toward Shug's Lexus. We'll see, he thought.

"I wouldn't make any accusations if I were you," Jimi said.

Mas winced but kept walking, a little slower now. Was that a threat?

"We wouldn't want you to lose another truck."

Mas stopped and turned. "Whatchu say?" He pictured the Ford, its hood scrunched like an accordion.

"We wouldn't want another mishap on Hecker Pass."

Mas felt like he couldn't breathe and clutched at the base of his throat. The bandage over his incision for the breathing tube was still there. Did Jimi cause the Ford to crash? "You…" he whispered. Seeing Mas's expression, Jimi took a few steps back.

"You!" He pushed out the word and flew at the old man,

tackling his legs and knocking the knife loose. Jimi went down like a felled old tree but didn't give up. He pulled first at some withered rhubarb leaves and then some dirt. Chunks of dark dirt were being pressed into Mas's eye sockets, his nostrils, his mouth. He struggled and squirmed, blowing soil out of his mouth and attempting to rub the dirt from his eyes. He still hung on to Jimi's leg, causing him to cry out in pain.

Mas then felt someone pulling him off of Jimi, actually lifting him up in the air.

It wasn't just one man, but three Jabami farmworkers wearing bandanas, as well as the field manager who Mas had seen earlier. "What the hell is going on here?" the manager asked no one in particular.

Jimi closed his fists and closed his mouth, silently vowing not to speak to anyone about poisoning Shug Arai. Mas Arai could have all his theories and accusations, but Jimi would provide no confessions. A confession would make it too easy. He would be whisked away in a police car; maybe even driven by Robin Arai. He could not let that happen, especially as long as Ats was alive.

After separating the two old men, the field hands and Jimi's manager gave up and walked away, obviously figuring that the conflict was rooted in a past they didn't understand.

Mas didn't have time to wash his face. He wiped himself with a rag, which only served to spread the dirt more evenly. He knew he looked a mess, which was confirmed when he entered Minnie's house again.

"Mas, what happened?" she cried.

"Minnie," he replied, "you'zu betta sit down."

CHAPTER THIRTEEN

Minnie, at first, didn't believe Mas. "Jimi Jabami? But he's an old man."

They all were old, but it was true. Jimi was even older than them.

"But how?"

"Poison. Rhubarb pie."

"I remember when Ats made that pie, long time ago. But none of us died."

"Dis time heavy duty," Mas said. It was the perfect crime, actually. He didn't know if the report Minnie was waiting for would be able to spot rhubarb poisoning.

"But why did Jimi want to kill Shug?"

"Jealousy. Jealousy ova new strawberry. Jealousy ova everytin'."

"This doesn't make any sense. After all these years, all these years of practically living side by side, going to temple together, Jimi secretly hated us? And what about Ats? She was like a sister to me, way back when."

"When Ats getsu sick, everytin' changed."

Minnie was quiet for a while. "I know Shug and I didn't go over there much. Is that why Jimi was mad? Because he thought we abandoned Ats?"

Mas shrugged his shoulders. "Don't make no sense. Heezu mad." And maybe if he were in Jimi's shoes, he'd be the same way. "Heezu want you to *kuro*."

"Suffer? But why?"

"Their family suffer, so Arais should, too."

"We're all going through hard times, Mas. I can't believe it. I just can't believe it."

Mas had a hard time accepting this as well. But Jimi had not only poisoned Shug, but he'd also destroyed the Ford in an attempt to destroy Mas. What Mas needed to figure out was what Jimi was going to do next.

Minnie peered into her half-empty coffee mug. Her shoulders drooped, just like her husband's once did. Perhaps she'd secretly hoped the killer was a stranger or maybe a business associate, a competitor. Not a fellow Nisei whom they had known for more than fifty years.

Jimi never really understood women like Minnie Arai, whom he knew as Minnie Nakamura before and in camp. They were the ones who always smiled, despite the dust blowing through the holes in their barracks or the coffin in front of them at a funeral.

His own mother released her list of discontents freely, so they flew out and formed a buttress, a wall between her and the outside world. He realized later that this was atypical for a Japanese woman of his mother's generation. Most of them buried their hurts and losses so deeply that sometimes their faces were sucked of all expressions of joy or even sadness.

But to mask that all with a smile? Wasn't that a bit demented? Jimi was afraid of those women. He did not trust them. He was convinced that they were quite dangerous, but how could he defend himself from them? He didn't own a gun, even a hunting gun. Ats had insisted that he get rid of all his weapons after they got married. When she was a girl, a seven-year-old neighbor boy was playing with his father's pistol while alone in the house. He accidentally discharged the gun, and Ats was the one who had found the boy's body, soaked in blood. *That would not happen to any of her children*, she said. No matter how much Jimi argued with her, the image of the boy could not be erased from her mind.

So there were no guns in the house. But there were plenty of kitchen knives, sharpened so meticulously that they could instantaneously slice a piece of paper. If that Mas Arai had opened his mouth—and he probably had—then the smiling widow would be coming after Jimi soon.

The closing of the front door woke Mas up. Then the sound of a deadbolt being slid into place and the running of a car engine. The digital clock on the dresser read two a.m. Mas put on a pair of Shug's pants and pulled down the blinds. Minnie's car was missing from the driveway. What was she up to? There weren't too many businesses in Watsonville that were open at that hour.

"Minnie," he called out, just to make sure. No response.

Walking in his stocking feet, he tried the front door. Wouldn't budge. He needed the key for the double lock, and when he went to the kitchen where the keys were hooked on the wall, he discovered that all of them were missing. Shug's

Lexus key, Minnie's Camry key, the extra house keys he was borrowing.

Mas shook his head clear of the nighttime cobwebs. No, no, it couldn't be. He rushed to the back door, but found the same thing—the deadbolt lock held him prisoner.

Why was Minnie keeping Mas captive in the house? It could only be one reason. He went into Shug's study and opened his desk drawer, the drawer that had held the gun. Of course, it was gone, too.

Mas considered calling Jimi. But why? That would only pave the way for Jimi to hurt Minnie with cause. Robin? He had her business card somewhere, but again, would he want to involve the police? Wouldn't that make it more difficult for Minnie?

Sonofagun. Mas circled the house, looking for somewhere to break out of the house. The double-pane windows made it difficult, plus it would leave such a mess, but he couldn't worry about that now.

He'd seen some golf clubs stored in a corner of Shug's study. He grabbed a nine-iron and went to the back, where a pretty window box displayed a row of violets. Not even bothering to remove the plants, Mas took a clean swing. The window shattered immediately, sending the pots of violets outside onto the ground. Grabbing some towels, Mas brushed away large pieces of glass and ducked his way outside.

Running around to the front, he surveyed his transportation options. He couldn't make it on foot. And then he remembered what the neighbor boy, Victor, had said— whenever you need a car. Mas went to find out if the offer was any good.

He saw her before she saw him. He was sitting at the kitchen table when he saw the glow of her car's headlights. The fog was thick that morning, so the beam had soft edges, like that of a distant star's, and then it shut off. She was coming.

Her hair was disheveled, and she wore a man's hunting jacket, maybe Shug's. He waited for her to ring the doorbell. Three times.

"Jiiimii," he heard Ats murmur down the hallway. *Ats, we will almost be there. Together, in nirvana.*

When Minnie drew out a gun in the open doorway, Jimi was not surprised. He had hoped for this.

He raised his hands instinctively, like they did in the television shows.

"Why? Just tell me why?" Jimi had always thought that Minnie was an attractive enough woman, but now he could see every line, crease, wrinkle. Not even Minnie was immune to the ravages of time. At least she wasn't smiling any more.

He silently backed away from Minnie and the gun, which he could see was shaking in her age-spotted hands. The skeleton hands and fingers with the prominent diamond ring. "Where is she?" she said, and then louder, "Where IS SHE?"

It became obvious to Jimi that Minnie wanted retribution. To avenge the poisoning of her husband, Minnie would shoot Ats. That was fine with Jimi, as long as he was next.

Walking backwards, he led her down the hall to Ats's bedroom.

The gun began to sag, and Jimi was afraid she would drop it. "Both hands, both hands."

She looked confused, yet she steadied the gun with both hands, as he suggested.

When they entered the bedroom, Minnie kept the gun on Jimi but turned her attention to Ats, who lay helplessly in her bed. She was awake but didn't seem to comprehend what was going on.

"Ats, oh, Ats. I haven't seen you in so long." The nose of the gun was aimed at the floor.

Just shoot her and then me. The mortgage insurance, while not covering suicides, would be applicable in a double homicide. "Shoot her," Jimi murmured and then louder, "Shoot her."

Minnie's hands shook and the gun with it. Ats's face turned to Jimi and for a moment, Jimi recognized an old familiar light in her eyes.

"Mmminnie," she mouthed. Jimi felt a streak of electricity go up his spine.

No, no, no, Jimi thought. *This will ruin everything.* He needed to think fast and think ugly. Say something that would keep Minnie's anger simmering and finally boil over enough for her to pull the trigger two times. "Shug used me, he used everyone around him," he said, meaning every word. "He used you, too. I'm sure I did you a favor."

She raised and pointed the gun right at him, and he could breathe again.

But he'd underestimated Minnie. "What are you trying to do?" she said. "Do you want me to kill you? Do you want me to destroy your life like you have destroyed mine?"

Too late, our lives are already destroyed, thought Jimi. He wondered how it would feel to enter the other world.

"Mmminnie." It was Ats again.

"Ats, shh." Jimi tried to control his voice. He didn't want his last words to his wife to be harsh.

"Is this why you killed him? Because you felt that we'd abandoned Ats?" Minnie's voice cracked as she spoke.

But you had, Jimi thought. *When she was young and active, you always had time for her, for us.* Coming around for free pies and cakes. Asking for donations, flats of strawberries, for the next temple fundraiser. The doorbell was always ringing for Ats. And she always answered, ready to fulfill any request. But apparently she wasn't needed anymore. And the quiet was slowly killing her.

"Ats, oh, Ats. What has become of us?" Minnie then slumped down to the floor, dropping the gun. Leaning against the wall, she covered her eyes. She started to make a strange noise, like a cat spitting out a hairball. Jimi finally realized that she was crying.

Ats pulled herself up with the bed railing and stared at Minnie.

"Goddammit," Jimi cursed. And then he cursed some more. Minnie kept crying and Ats kept watching. "You know, you Arais, you have it all. Money, everyone knows you and respects you. Trips around the world. The Stem House."

More crying and hiccupping. Tears were also running down Ats's face. Did she understand what was happening?

Minnie wiped her nose on the cuff of the jacket, which obviously was too large for her. "What are you talking about? We don't have the Stem House anymore."

"That's your son's stupidity. Finally caught up with him."

Minnie's mouth took on an ugly shape. "Shug took all

the money. All our retirement money. I have nothing. I may even lose the house we are living in."

"But how can that be?"

"He put it all into the new strawberry. Every single penny. I curse that new berry."

Jimi sunk back onto the wall. *What?* His mind whirled, trying to make sense of Minnie's revelation.

The screen door screeched open and shut, and a new person entered Ats's small room. Mas must have been running, because his chest was heaving up and down. Seeing Minnie on the floor next to the gun, he took a fighting stance. "Whatchu do?" he demanded of Jimi.

"You need to take her home."

"Sonofabitch." Mas raised his fist to strike the old man.

Minnie stopped him. "No, Mas, no. It wasn't him. It was me. I was going to kill Ats. Like he killed Shug."

Mas felt like a top that was losing steam. Outside, the sirens of the police cars sounded louder and louder until their wailing finally ceased a few yards away.

Mas feared that the police would cart away Minnie. If so, it would all be his fault. Because he, after all, was behind the call to the police. It had been the patriarch of the Duran House, the housebound Miguel, who had insisted on informing the police before he'd give up the keys to the Impala.

It looked mighty suspicious, the gun in the middle of the room next to Minnie. They were frozen in place from either fear or shock, all of them except for Ats. She had jumped over her bed rail and scooped up the weapon, slipping it underneath her mattress. Then magically she was back in bed, wrapped back in her sheets, mummified.

The officer who Mas had met at his motel room break-in was first on the scene. "We got a report that there might be possible shooting at this address," he said, a gun in his hands.

"I did it," Jimi bleated, shocking both Mas and Minnie. "I'm the one who killed her husband."

As soon as he said those words, Jimi felt he had found his solution. *I killed Shug Arai.* Four simple words. The police asked him the same questions forty different ways. The same answer: *I killed Shug Arai.* They wanted details—how he had done it, when he had started to plan to kill him—but all Jimi could give them was, *I killed Shug Arai.* They brought in a Japanese interpreter, obviously hoping that a different language would stir a different, more detailed response. But it was the same, *I killed Shug Arai.* On a yellow lined pad of paper, Jimi carefully held the pen and wrote over and over again, *I killed Shug Arai.*

He felt the authorities growing frustrated. Some of the experts even raised their voices and threatened him, his family. But Jimi felt like he was floating over the police station, the chimneys, the city, the farmlands. He was up in the night clouds, feeling moisture soak into the wrinkles of his face, caressing his dry, gray hair and the stubble on his chin and underneath his nose. His best defense was the truth, a truth that they could not prove. He was untouchable.

CHAPTER FOURTEEN

I don't understand," Minnie told the assistant district attorney, a harmless-looking man who apparently had just gotten promoted. "He's confessed. How can he already be released? Why hasn't he been charged with my husband's murder?"

The attorney had a nervous habit of brushing down an imaginary moustache underneath his nose. Mas moved his weight from one side of his body to the other. He and Minnie sat in the attorney's crammed office, files stacked on all sides of the desk, threatening to topple over them both.

"His attorney said that he confessed under duress. He's eighty years old and is the main caregiver for his terminally ill wife. He's a sympathetic figure, that's for sure."

"But this toxicology report. . . ." Minnie waved an envelope in front of the attorney's nose. She'd been waving it in front of everyone since she received it in the mail that morning. "It says right here that there was a high level, a dangerously high level, of oxalic acid in my husband's body. Rhubarb leaves have oxalic acid."

"Yes, but so does black tea. Also certain bacteria can produce it as well." He turned to Mas. "I was a chemistry major in college." Mas was unimpressed. The attorney cleared his throat. "The thing is, it's not illegal for someone to be growing rhubarb. I mean, if we were talking about a poisoning with an illicit drug, it would be a different story."

"How about Linus? He's said that Shug ate a pie the day before he died. A pie made by Jimi Jabami. And that he wasn't feeling well afterward."

"I know, that's something, for sure. But it still doesn't prove that Mr. Jabami killed your husband."

"What do we need? What do we need to prosecute him?"

"Well, if he told someone his plan. Or if he gives the sheriff a proper confession, with specific details on how and why he poisoned your husband."

"And without that?" Minnie asked.

"I'm sorry," the attorney said. "There's not much I can do."

"I can't believe it," Minnie said after she and Mas had given their lunch orders to the waitress at the coffee shop down the street from the courthouse. Sitting across from her, Mas noticed how exhausted Minnie looked. Her face, devoid of any makeup, was the color of dirty dishwater.

"I still can't believe it," she repeated. "Jimi will be out there, free as a bird, after what he's done. If I hadn't left Shug alone, this never would have happened. He didn't want me to go to Santa Maria and leave him behind. Shug may have seemed so independent, but he relied on me." Minnie started sniffling, enough to warrant taking a tissue from her purse.

Mas felt that he had failed Minnie and Shug. Yes, he'd helped find Shug's killer, but what did it matter if Jimi wasn't going to pay for his crime? All that was left was a pang of emptiness. The waitress, too friendly for their mood, delivered their overflowing plates and refreshed their coffee cups. They picked at their food and spoke about nothing significant for a while.

Finally, Mas had to deliver the news. "I'zu gotta get back to Rosu Angelesu."

Minnie nodded. "I know. You've done so much for us already. Even if Jimi's out there free, at least I know, and he knows that I know. Even that much is a great relief to me."

Minnie excused herself to go to the bathroom, leaving Mas with his half-eaten tuna melt and cold French fries. As he reached for his coffee, he heard hard soles approaching. Someone moved into the seat across from him. Instead of Minnie in a fleece jacket, it was a uniformed sergeant, the very same Arturo Salgado from Laila's murder scene, with a radio wrapped around his shoulder like a snake.

Before Mas could react, Sergeant Salgado began talking. "I have some more questions for you."

Mas glanced at the tops of graying heads in the coffee shop. *Where was Minnie?*

Salgado must have read his mind. "She's still talking to a friend by the women's bathroom. She probably won't be back for a while," he said. "I just wanted to give you a chance to speak the truth."

Mas tightened his grip on his fork.

"I can wait until Billy's mother returns to the booth."

Minnie had been through so much over the past forty-eight hours. She didn't need this so-called detective further ruining her lunch.

Mas sighed and nodded. He was ready to face anything the sergeant was going to shovel his way.

"We haven't found the murder weapon yet. Nothing in the greenhouse matched Laila's injury. It was quite a blow to the head. Splinters of wood. Maybe by a wooden pole. A bat."

As soon as he heard "bat," Mas felt like he might shrink in his shoes, right then and there. He thought, of course, about the bat carved by Wataru Arai. Conveniently placed in the casket and now buried in a cemetery plot in Watsonville. Who had the opportunity to put the bat in the casket? Billy was first on the list. Then, of course, Minnie, her daughters, and Billy's children. Who knows—maybe Oily and Evelyn had the opportunity, too. Regardless, it would have to be someone who knew that the bat had a special significance to the Arai family's legacy. Chances were, too, that it was someone that Mas knew.

Sergeant Salgado intently studied Mas's face. "You wouldn't know of any bats in the greenhouse?"

Mas wadded up a napkin. "No, nuttin'. Been away ova fifty years."

"I also just heard about the new variety Sugarberry is planning to introduce."

Mas felt a coolness at back of his neck.

"It's called the Masao. Quite a coincidence. Isn't your birth name Masao?"

The fact that Salgado had been checking into his identity troubled Mas. What did he know that Mas didn't?

"Thatsu Shug's bizness. Strawberry bizness. I'zu just a gardener from Rosu Angelesu."

"No, Mr. Arai, you are not 'just' anything."

They both noticed Minnie making her way back to the booth.

"Well," he said, standing up. "You know where to find me. If you need to tell me something." He then went to greet a couple sitting at a nearby table.

Minnie's reaction was immediate. "What did he want?"

"Nuttin'," Mas lied. " Just wanted to getsu some salt."

As soon as he drove Minnie home, Mas headed to the guest room for a nap. But the problem was that he couldn't sleep. He tossed and turned on the twin bed, thinking about bloody baseball bats, poisonous rhubarb leaves, and strawberries worth killing for. By the time he was ready to leave Watsonville, he'd hoped that Minnie would feel safer. But now the exact opposite had happened.

He stumbled out of the room into the hallway, which had the whiff of something sweet baking.

A photo album lay open on the living room table. Black-and-white prints, attached meticulously with photo corners.

"I found more photos of you with Shug," Minnie called out from the kitchen. "Before you left, I thought you might want to see them."

Mas fingered the thick, black album paper. Each page had a different story. The gang clam digging in Pismo Beach, picnicking with rice balls and sandwiches at Point Lobos, picking wild berries in the mountains. In every shot, Shug and Mas were smiling. Mas couldn't remember a time when he smiled so much.

Minnie sat down with a plate of warm cookies and turned the album page. "Oh, here you are at UC Davis.

I didn't know you visited Shug in college."

There were the three of them, Oily, Shug, and Mas. Mas had his long sleeves rolled up to his upper arm, a simple bandage covering the place where a scalpel had claimed an inch of skin. Both he and Oily were playfully making biceps like Popeye, while Shug, his trademark glasses overwhelming his narrow face, was bent over laughing.

Minnie pointed to Mas's bandages. "What was that for?" she asked.

Some research project, wasn't that what Shug had told them? He didn't give many details.

Mas reached for the magnifying loupe that was always on hand when Minnie was examining her photo albums. The sign on the department building was now readable. Genetics.

If Shug was in the photo, then who had taken it in the first place? Mas's mind raced back fifty years. There was that strange *hakujin* boy, one of Shug's classmates. He was small in stature like them. Mas couldn't remember much what he looked like. Only that he prided himself in being what he called, what was it again, naturally, nature man, nature-ist? Basically he liked to walk around in the nude.

"Mas, are you alright? You look like you've seen a ghost."

"The otha scientist at Sugarberry, Shug's friend?"

"Who? Linus Verdorben?"

Mas nodded. "He at Davis, too?"

"Yes, they were in the same class." Minnie frowned. "Why do you ask?"

A sign-waving crowd, even larger than usual, blocked the Sugarberry driveway. The protesters' message had changed ever so slightly; it now was based on the strawberry commission's meeting that was scheduled the next day. The chants, however, were pretty much the same. Mas noticed one large difference, which was also noted by another protester, one of those bedraggled *hakujin* college students he'd seen at the earlier meeting.

"Rosa not here?"

"She hasn't been here the whole week."

"Why?"

"I dunno. Elias is pissed about it. Says that she's not telling everyone what she knows."

Mas slipped through the crowd, anonymous as usual. Where was Rosa? He needed to talk to her. She was supposed to hear from Laila's friend, the scientist, about the Masao berry, wasn't she?

Just as Rosa was MIA from the protest line at Sugarberry, her daughter Cecilia was absent from the motel. Mas wandered through the three main floors, even attempting to go to the fourth floor, but at the top of the stairs, a locked gate barred his entry. A sign hung from a knob: PRIVATE PARTY.

What was it with this fourth floor? Mas wondered, remembering the sound of Cecilia's high heels on her way up there.

Through the gate, Mas could see a swimming pool with a few rooms surrounding it. He also spied something on the ground outside the gate. It was smooth and black, appropriately called *ishi*, or "stone" in Japanese. But this wasn't an everyday stone; no, it was a *go* piece imprinted with the Japanese character for forever, *eien*.

Forever Inn, wasn't this the name of the motel? And then there was Forever Resort across the street from the Everbears headquarters. This was more than a coincidence. This place must be owned by Clay Gorman.

Mas heard something by the far side of the pool and pressed his face against the gate's grating. Two figures, most likely men, emerged from one of the rooms.

"How many tonight?"

"Just five. Do we have enough girls?" The thin, monotone voice was a familiar one. It came from a skinny body in a long sleeved t-shirt and jeans. Clay Gorman.

"Kekai won't help us anymore. And that sorority at UC Santa Cruz is having some function tonight."

"Damn."

A door opened from another room and Mas immediately recognized the outline of a mass of long, curly hair—Cecilia. She had some folded towels in her arms. By now, Mas had also identified the other man as Scott, the desk clerk.

"Hey, Cecilia, could you get some of your college friends to stop by tonight?" Clay asked.

"They're not interested, and they won't do it for the money. Most of them have boyfriends. My boyfriend wants me to stop, too."

"It's not like you're prostitutes."

"I know, I know, we are hostesses. But some of your friends did some inappropriate things last time."

"Those weren't my friends. They were some venture capitalists from San Diego. I barely knew them. These ones tonight won't do anything, I swear."

"I don't know, Mr. Gorman. My mother's been pretty upset lately. You know, with everything. I think I should spend some time with her tonight."

"Well, you have to do what you have to do. At least let's get some of the good wine out. Scott, what do we have left from last time?"

"Not sure."

"I'll go down with you and check out what we have. Meanwhile, Cecilia, can you clean out the ashtrays?"

The two men started walking toward the gate, and Mas hurried around the corner and stood behind a potted ficus tree. The gate clanged open and Mas watched as Clay and the desk clerk made their way down the stairs.

The gate hadn't properly closed, so Mas slipped in. He watched Cecilia in her maid's apron filling a bucket with water from a hose. It took her a minute before she noticed Mas standing there by the pool.

"What are you doing here?" The hose fell out of her hand and was spilling water onto the patio. A large stone barbecue pit was surrounded by padded deck chairs. On a platform was an impressive *go* board, essentially a grid of lines on a wooden pedestal, and two bowls filled with *ishi*, one all white and the other all black.

"I findsu dis," Mas said, placing the black stone on the *go* board.

"You shouldn't be here. The owner won't like it." Cecilia turned off the water.

"Whatchu doin'? Sumptin police won't like?"

"No, nothing like that. It's just a party. A private pool

party for some people who may invest in our area."

Mas remembered how Billy said he'd met Laila at a pool party thrown by Clay. Had it been here? "How Laila involve?"

Cecilia sighed. "Okay, if I tell you, will you leave?"

Mas nodded.

"Laila wasn't 'involved.' It was her younger sister, Kekai. She used to get her friends from Santa Cruz to come over and go swimming. They were just supposed to talk to Mr. Gorman's friends. Nothing more. But Laila found out and went ballistic. She came here and started yelling at Mr. Gorman during one of his parties. Kekai was so embarrassed. I think she had a little crush on Mr. Gorman. After that, she stopped coming here."

A blast of synthesized beats sounded from Cecilia's apron pocket. She pulled out a cell phone and frowned as she looked at the display.

Holding the phone to her ear, she said, "I'm fine, Mom. I'm here at work. Why do you need me to be home? Stop being so paranoid." She said a few more words and put the phone back in her pocket.

"Ohmygod, what's going on today?" she said almost to herself. "You're asking me questions about Laila. Mom's been in hysterics, saying that whatever happened to Laila may happen to her."

Mas jerked his head up.

"I think she's going through some hormonal changes. She's been acting so strange. Getting mysterious packages, secret calls. You'd think she joined the CIA or something. And then yesterday, I come home and this old white man with a beard takes off from the house."

Mas waited. "Boyfriend?"

"Oh no, nothing like that. I mean, she wouldn't tell me who he was. But I have a hunch it has something to do with strawberries. He drove off in a truck with a Sugarberry logo on its side."

Jimi Jabami should have felt victorious. He had beaten the legal system, beaten the Arai family. But then there was Ats. Her body had gotten weaker, but her mind, sharper. Her face had become gaunt, with hollow cheeks. She could no longer speak with her voice, but she could still speak with her eyes. And her eyes were not happy with him right now.

Over the years, they did have their disagreements, mostly before the children arrived. When it came to their children, they were unified, in total agreement. When the first child, a girl, was born, Jimi finally felt that his blood family was being restored. All the hardness from past losses could soften a bit, or at least be sidelined temporarily.

One of their early arguments during their marriage was actually over Mas Arai. He had been arrested in Salinas for a minor theft, and Ats wanted to bail him out.

"Why? Let his people do it." By people, Jimi meant, of course, the Arais.

"He's alone," Ats insisted. She didn't care how many distant relatives he had in this country. She herself was alone after her parents had repatriated from Tule Lake to Japan immediately after the war. Not the types to forgive and forget, Ats's father and mother had answered "no, no" to the so-called loyalty questionnaire. Ats, their oldest daughter and almost eighteen, insisted on staying behind.

Some Nisei, especially those who had volunteered for the U.S. Army, disapproved of the stance taken by Ats's parents. Jimi, on the other hand, admired their gumption. This same gumption was part of Ats's genetic makeup. She knew how to stand her ground, and she stood her ground regarding Mas and his bail money.

"He's going to have to work it off. Every bit of it, including interest," Jimi said to his young wife as she got into the driver's seat of a truck owned by Jabami Farms. He could still remember what she was wearing—a yellow sweater, her favorite at the time, over a cotton dress with tiny flowers. At that moment, Jimi had marveled at what a lucky man he was.

The doorbell then rang, causing Jimi to turn to the window facing Ats's hospital bed. He saw a Sugarberry truck parked along their dirt path. He went to the front door to let his visitor in.

CHAPTER FIFTEEN

Before Mas left Watsonville for Los Angeles in 1950, Shug came down to Sacramento to say goodbye.

"We've had some good times over here, haven't we?" Mas didn't know what to say. After Shug left for college, he had rarely heard from him. Yes, Shug had invited him and Oily early on, but it seemed to be just to participate in some kind of scientific study. Shug never told them what had happened with the blood and tissue he'd collected.

The last time Mas spoke to him, Shug had asked his opinion about Minnie.

"Sheezu nice girl," Mas said. Minnie was indeed pleasant, a ready smile on her face. She had stayed in Watsonville and was taking teaching classes at the local junior college.

"Evelyn is sure ready to get married," Shug said.

"Good for her," Mas answered. And he meant it. He just didn't want to be the fish caught in her net. He figured his move to Southern California would put an end to her advances.

"What are you planning to do in Los Angeles?"

"Gardenin'."

"A lot of Nisei are getting into that in the big cities. You'll do well."

Mas swallowed and nodded. But nothing like how well you will be doing, he thought. Shug was smart and was on his way to getting a degree from UC Davis. They were on two different tracks, headed for separate futures.

"We'll stay in touch," Shug said.

And they did. Christmas cards, purchased at holiday sales a day after the previous Christmas. Minnie signed for "The Arais." And Chizuko signed theirs.

Aside from seeing each other at the occasional funeral, that had been the extent of their intimacy over the past forty years. So Mas had been puzzled, of course, about why Shug would immortalize him with his groundbreaking strawberry, the Masao. But now it was becoming clearer.

Mas attempted to reach her over the phone, but she hung up the second she heard his voice. So he had to make a face-to-face visit instead. The neighborhood was familiar, an old one, just a block past the Buddhist temple. The home was a simple one-story wood-framed house that couldn't be much larger than eight hundred square feet.

The tiny house had many windows, at least two on every side. Even the door had a glass panel. And today each of the windows was covered, with shades drawn tightly. Mas rapped his knuckles on the door.

The curtains on the door pulled back, revealing fingers wrapped around a shotgun. Rosa's voice was surprisingly clear through the glass. "I have a license for this. And I know how to use it."

Mas took a few steps away from the door and turned back toward the walkway. Then came the jangle of a chain being slid back and the popping open of the door.

"Wait," she commanded. Mas complied.

"Nobody seen youzu at Sugarberry," Mas spoke with his back turned to Rosa.

"I bet everyone's relieved about that."

"Whyzu you been away?"

Now was not the time for her to be *moku-moku*, quiet. Mas turned around to look at Rosa, face-to-face. She was wearing a black cotton shirt and cargo pants. She looked as if she hadn't slept all night. "You knowsu about the new strawberry."

"What are you talking about?"

"You knowsu. I knowsu."

Still cradling the shotgun, Rosa gestured toward her house. "Get in," she said, "before I change my mind."

With thick curtains over the windows and no light, the house was as dark as the mood of its inhabitant. Rosa started pacing, causing the wooden floorboards to squeak. "How can you know about the Masao? You're still standing. Alive. Laila's dead. Her friend who analyzed the Masao is scared to death."

Mas frowned.

Rosa stopped pacing. "Yeah, yeah. She's been getting death threats, anonymous ones, but we know who they're from. And now he's threatening to hurt Cecilia if I open my mouth. He keeps saying that this is going to save the strawberry industry, that it's going to help a lot of people, but he's not thinking about the people who'll be buying and eating the Masao. He's crazy. He's nuts. And that's why I'm afraid he might follow through with his threats."

Rosa stopped to listen to the sounds of children playing in the street for a minute. "Anyway, I don't know how he found out about me in the first place. Did you say anything to anyone about me contacting the lab?"

"No, no don't say nuttin'," Mas quickly replied, not sure if he had or not.

"Youzu sure he killed Laila?" he asked.

"Who else would have?"

Mas went to where he last saw Shug alone, at least when his friend was dead. The mortuary was hushed, a few loose dead leaves falling onto the walkway. He spotted a few dandelions in corners of the lawn. Weeds seemed to be the only new things alive at the mortuary today.

The front door opened easily. No one was in the front room, but a tall dark-haired woman appeared from the back. "Can I help you?" She had an easy voice, a voice that a man could tell his problems to.

"I'zu Shug Arai's relative," he introduced himself.

"Oh, I'm so sorry. I believe I recognize you from the visitation. You came early that day."

Mas was shocked that the woman would have remembered him. With a bunch of Nisei men about the same height and weight, it took a pretty discerning *hakujin* woman to tell them apart.

"I'zu just have question for you."

"Of course." The woman was eager to please, so Mas continued.

"Baseball bat, there'su one dat was in the casket."

"Yes, yes, I already spoke to the detective about that. . . ."

"Robin Arai?"

"No, no, Sergeant Salgado. From the Watsonville Police. Like I told him, I have no idea who put that bat in the casket. I just assumed it was a member of the family; I mean, no one asked me about it at the time."

"Not there on Friday."

The woman nodded, blinking rapidly. "Yes, I don't remember it being placed on the visitation day, either. It must have been the day of the funeral. I was here early, around seven-thirty, on that Saturday to prepare for another funeral. I didn't notice anyone come in. We don't have a problem with theft in this place, as you can well imagine. I mean, it's quite conceivable that a loved one came in and left the memento in the casket. People do strange things when they're in mourning." The woman fingered a stray piece of hair and pulled it back behind her ear. "Was the bat valuable? Is that why so many people are interested in it?"

Mas didn't answer and looked out the window. More leaves were falling from the ash tree. "You'zu tree is a bit sick," he told her. "When the gardener come around?"

"On Saturday mornings," she said.

"Can I getsu his phone numba?" Mas said. "I can maybe tellsu him what to do."

One thing about an Impala, you could drive a lot faster in it than in a 1956 Ford truck that was literally duct-taped together. Mas leaned into the curves of the road, not caring if the Highway Patrol noticed that he was going twenty miles over the speed limit. Let them come. Let them all come to Castroville.

Linus's truck was parked by his mural-covered trailer, but Mas didn't care. He headed straight for the fields, for the experimental crops that were behind a ten-foot-high barbed-wire fence. The entryway was locked—if only Mas had his Ford, filled with his tools, he would have had an easier way in. The Impala's trunk only revealed a dirty blanket, empty water bottles, a tire iron, a baseball, and a spare tire—nothing that could do any damage to the barbed-wire fence. Mas examined the lock on Linus's garage—that one also required a good pair of bolt cutters.

The Impala was shiny and freshly washed—he hated to do this, but he felt he had no other choice. Sitting in the vinyl driver's seat, he moved the car so it faced the fence. Pulling the hand brake, he floored the gas pedal and then released the brake handle. The Impala lurched forward, the nose of the car crashing down the fence.

Next came the picking. He bent down toward the strawberry plants, his back remembering the same movement from decades ago. But instead of gently plucking each red jewel of fruit to place in a crate, Mas began tearing at the plants, pulling them from their roots and stomping on the fruit. He repeated this, dumping tangled vines in a pile.

He was destroying the third row of plants when Linus came out in his sarong, carrying a lawn chair and umbrella. He set up a shady seat a few yards from the uprooted fence and watched, sipping something exotic from a dark bottle.

Sweat washed down from Mas's forehead, and he stopped for a moment to wipe the wetness away with his shirt sleeve.

"Would you like some kind of refreshment after all that work?" Linus finally called out.

Mas actually would have, but he would have never accepted a drink from Linus Verdorben.

"Thank you for picking these strawberries." Linus rose from his seat and gingerly stepped on the downed chain-link fence in his sandals. He walked to the pile of plants and tugged at a strawberry that Mas had missed, popping it into his mouth.

"Tasty. Sweet as can be."

Hearing that syrupy comment, Mas almost gagged.

"The sweetness is compliments of the berry created by Jimi Jabami's and Shug's fathers. They called it the Taro after some folktale. Quaint, huh? I believe it's called Mimi-taro or something like that."

Momo-taro, you *bakatare*, Mas silently corrected.

"Anyway, the Taro was slow to produce. Shug still thought he could do something with them. He saw their potential."

Linus chewed slowly as he spoke, as if he were savoring each bite. "And then, lo and behold, we were experimenting with crossing the plant with other varieties. And then one night—I have to admit Jack Daniels was involved—Shug had a wild idea."

Mas felt light-headed, as if he were close to fainting.

"Your cells were very interesting. We've been watching them over the years. While samples from others just sat there, yours exploded. Yours grow in double, triple the time.

We considered the fact that you were exposed to heavy doses of radiation during the atomic bombing. Perhaps more radiation means more reproduction. That got Shug wondering—what if we could combine this power of reproduction with the sweetness of the Taro?"

Something began to stir in Masao. Shock turned into anger, not only toward Linus, but also toward Shug. How could Shug, who had known him from age eighteen, betray him like this?

"It wasn't instantaneous. It took several tries and, of course, multiple generations. Maybe even thirty. Some earlier varieties were even grown at the Stem House. With each generation, the berry got firmer. And then the perfect one was born this year. Right here. The Masao. Beautiful fruit, fast reproduction, long shelf life. And get this—now we find out that the Masao is resistant to disease, fights off strawberry yellows, can you believe it?"

Mas couldn't stand it any longer. "You'zu can't do dis. Neva gave permission for sumptin like dis."

"Well, you gave your cells a long time ago. Before we started having any kind of protocols. And yes, they are your cells. The DNA from your toothbrush proves it."

The missing toothbrush. It hadn't been lost in the hubbub of the break-in; it was the purpose of the break-in.

Mas was desperate for anything that might stop Linus. He gestured toward the destroyed plants. "All your Masaos gone now."

Linus laughed. "You're a gardener yourself, aren't you, Mas? Then you know that strawberries go back to their mothers. And these, my friend, are just the daughters, not the mothers. The mothers are safe and sound."

"I tellsu everyone. I tellsu them that I'zu the Masao."

"No, you won't. I've been studying you, Mas. You're a private man. A quiet man. Once the Masao comes out and you come forward, saying that your cells are in the strawberry, do you know what's going to happen?"

You'll be ruined, thought Mas.

"The tabloid reporters will be camped out in front of your house in Altadena. There will be TV media from all around the world wanting to interview the man who was turned into a strawberry."

Mas tried not to fall over. What Linus was saying was true. He could imagine Mari and his grandson struggling to get through a crowd of reporters, the photographs, the video cameras. How could he let that happen to himself, his family? He knew that he was completely outplayed, beaten.

"Well, if you'll excuse me, I have a big day tomorrow. Shug was supposed to be the one making the presentation at the strawberry commission meeting tomorrow. With him gone, I'll have to introduce the Masao to the world."

CHAPTER SIXTEEN

Shug wouldn't have done that to you, Mas. He wouldn't do that to any human being," Minnie said after Mas explained about the genesis of the Masao.

"No, no, he do it." Mas now remembered going into the Davis laboratory. It was small, with linoleum floors and wooden cabinets. Linus was taking a blood sample from Oily. "Oooowwww," Oily exclaimed. "That hurts." A hundred-and-seventy-pound baby.

With Mas, it was a little different. Shug was almost excited to see the raised mole by Mas's elbow. "I just want to take a specimen of this. It won't hurt much, I promise." Shug rubbed something yellowish-red on the mole—it almost started to tingle—then picked up a scalpel, as sharp and menacing as a barbershop razor.

"You'zu know what you'zu doin'?" Mas asked.

"I've been doing this all semester, Mas. No worries." His glasses were a little askew, and his right eye looked slightly magnified.

"Look away, Mas," Oily said, a bandage around his bicep.

And there, the bump was sliced away and placed in a clear container.

"He do it. He do it," Mas insisted.

"I don't believe it."

Then why? Why the Masao? Why was this *bakatare* strawberry named after him?

Minnie refused to believe what Shug did and excused herself. "I need to lie down for a while," she said.

Well, what about me, Mas thought. He couldn't stay under Shug's roof one minute longer. He didn't feel right wearing Shug's clothes anymore, so he opted for his only available outfit, the funeral suit and hard shoes. Before leaving the neighorhood, he made one phone call and placed a check for the Impala in the mail slot of the Duran house.

He would check back into the motel, but before that, he needed to make a stop in a familiar old neighborhood not far from the cemetery where the pioneers of Watsonville were buried.

The gardener only had a few tools in his bare bones old pickup truck, parked underneath an oak tree: a Makita lawnmower circa 1990 (should be secured down with a locked chain, thought Mas), a worn-out rake, and an old-fashioned edger. This gardener was definitely a rookie, a one-man show. And he couldn't speak a lick of English— well, maybe he could manage at least one lick. His son had warned Mas as much over the phone; this was after revealing that the gardener could be found at this duplex not far from Rosa's house.

"Hallo," Mas greeted the gardener, who glared suspiciously at Mas's suit and vehicle.

Mas had written down the address of the mortuary on the back of a business card in his wallet, and now he showed it to the gardener, who last name was Ramirez.

Ramirez squinted at the address. "Ya, my customa."

Mas wrote down the date of the funeral. He tried to remember the beginning Spanish from his junior college class,

taken to improve his communication with his various help-
ers. "*Domingo*, no, *sabado*. *Sabado*," Mas said proudly.

"Sa-tur-day?"

"Yah, Saturday morning."

Mas proceeded with a series of gestures. He stretched
out his arms about three feet and then, clasping his hands
together, simulated the swing of a baseball bat.

Ramirez scratched his head, forcing Mas to do his pre-
tend swing a couple of times.

"Ah-ya, ya, ya. Baseball bat," Ramirez finally said, breaking out in a smile.

"Who take inside?"

"Ya, ya. I rememba. *Chiquita bonita.*"

Once he was settled in his new motel room, this time on the
second floor, Mas found himself wishing for some advice.
He went to the telephone—he knew the number by heart.
Genessee Howard's.

Genessee stayed quiet while Mas reported as best as he
could what Shug had done to him. "And itsu called Masao.
Probably to shut my mouth." Because who would want to
lay claim to being inside a strawberry?

Halfway through their conversation, the dam broke. The
deluge began.

"This is criminal!" Mas had never heard Genessee's voice
so high-pitched. "This is an invasion of your civil rights!
They can't just take your DNA and use it in a food product
that they're going to sell to thousands of people! And what if

the public finds out about it? You'll never hear the end of it. What were they thinking?"

Now it was Mas's turn to listen without saying a word.

Jimi Jabami woke up feeling like a new man. He was able to pay the mortgage on the farm this month, plus the past six months of monies that he owed, thanks to the deal he'd made with Linus Verdorben. There was no need now to hasten the demise of Ats's life, not to mention his. He had a lot to look forward to, in fact. Today he would be introduced to all the strawberry growers and the commission as a new addition to Sugarberry's staff. Barely finishing high school and never going to college, he would achieve his dream. He would become a breeder.

Jimi didn't realize that the title would mean so much to him, but it did. He tried to imagine the expressions on Minnie's and Billy's faces. *My name will be on patents, just like Shug's was.* He wouldn't merely be a farmer, a founding member of a cooperative, but a member of the scientific community. Here was his chance to resurrect the Taro. Perhaps use the Masao, but combine it with some of Sugarberry's older varieties. He could become a master chef—not with the cooking or grilling of food, but rather creating it. He could not wait to begin his new life.

Like almost every other structure involving farming in the

area, the strawberry commission's building was completely forgettable. Gray, dirt-colored bricks stacked into a giant rectangular box. The parking lot, at least, had been recently repaved, its black surface the color of the outside of an Oreo cookie. Most of the spots were taken, but Mas was lucky enough to find something toward the front, next to a television van with long antennae protruding from its roof.

"What did you do to Lupita?" Victor, wearing his trademark hoodie sweatshirt, stood in front of the Impala.

"Lupita?"

"My car." Victor stared sadly at the deep scratches on the once-shiny brown paint on the Impala's hood.

"Dis not your car anymore." Lupita? Mas couldn't stand people who named their cars. He vowed that his Impala would be released of any past silly attachments.

Mas ignored Victor and left the boy to cry over the damage; he had no time for it on today of all days.

A half a dozen uniformed officers stood by the door, facing what looked like the same group of protesters who had been at Sugarberry. Yes, there was the same girl with the macramé hat, the same Latino man with a shaved head and a goatee. Most of them were carrying signs: SAFE WORKERS, SAFE BERRIES. One woman started to chant, and after a few awkward tries, she finally got several of them to peal out the same out-of-tune protest refrain.

As the crowd grew more animated, a few of the policemen clutched at their batons.

Watching on the sidelines was Robin Arai.

"You're still here," she said to Mas, her sunglasses following the protesters.

From the time Mas had first met her, two weeks ago, Robin somehow looked thinner. Her cheekbones seemed more prominent, and even her graying hair, again pulled back in a bun, appeared less full.

Mas stood next to her for a while. She didn't seem happy to have the company. A group of young uniformed officers walked by and, noticing Robin, greeted her with congenial messages.

"We'll miss you, lieutenant."

"Good luck."

Mas waited until the officers disappeared inside the building. "Youzu goin' somewhere?"

"I'm taking early retirement. It's something I've been thinking of for a long time. Everything with Uncle Shug has shown me that life is too short."

Yes, Mas thought, *yes, indeed.*

"Howsu the girlu, Alyssa?"

"Fine. Back at school. Why do you ask?" Finally the sunglasses turned to Mas. Before they stayed on him too long, he ducked his head and left for the press conference.

Inside, people were crammed into the hospital-white room. In the back, standing on a platform, were cameramen from local television stations, their equipment set on tripods. Folding chairs, which must have at one time been organized in straight lines and rows, had been moved to form clusters of cliques, each most likely representing various strawberry-growing cooperatives and companies, which could be identified by the color-coordinated polo shirts on the employees. A podium stood at the front of the room, arranged next to a long table with name cards that clearly read, "Billy Arai," "Clay Gorman," and "Linus Verdorben." If the meeting had occurred a month earlier, Shug Arai's name would have been there as well.

More than ever, Mas felt out of place. Before he could make a move for the exit, someone pushed him into the hallway next to the men's bathroom.

"Do you know what's going on? The *San Jose Mercury-News* is here. *Christian Science Monitor.* Associated Press. And a few local network TV reporters." Billy Arai had gotten a haircut, which made him look all-American. That was good, Mas thought. After this was over, he might be viewed as the normal Arai.

"You'zu find out."

"No, you tell me."

"I'zu the Masao."

"Yes, I know that Sugarberry's variety is called the Masao."

"No, no, I'zu the Masao. My cells in there."

"What?" Billy was beginning to laugh.

This was no laughing matter. "I'zu the Masao."

"No." Billy folded his arms. "No."

Mas could only manage a nod of his head.

"But how?"

"At college, Shug cutsu off dis bump on my arm. Neva tole me whatsu gonna happen with it."

"Linus put him up to this. It was Linus."

Although Mas knew that Linus was capable of the most

heinous of crimes, he knew the creation of the Masao was definitely Shug's brainchild.

"I can't believe it. I can't believe it."

When Billy then learned that Mas was determined to talk to the reporters, he became desperate. "So what? You're going to tell everyone that your cells are in the Masao? That's suicide, Mas. Everyone will be after you. You'll be labeled a freak, a monster. And my father will be Doctor Frankenstein."

Mas knew what he was risking, sacrificing. His life, as he knew it, would be ending. He was like a *kamikaze* pilot, steering his plane into the enemy. Mas knew no other way to stop Linus Verdorben.

"Billy," someone interrupted. Clay Gorman, who had finally combed his hair, whispered something in Billy's ear.

"I need to get ready," Billy told Mas. He shook his head. "I hope you know what you're doing."

After the two men left for the front of the room, Mas stood beside the cameramen's platform in the back. He was petrified. His hands felt clammy, and he thought he would pass out right then and there. He couldn't believe that in less than an hour, he'd be on the other side of those cameras, announcing that he was more a part of the Masao strawberry than he cared to imagine. The news would spread like a flash from television camera to computer and cell phone. All of Watsonville's finest were here to witness it in person—or almost all. There were a few absentees.

For instance, no Minnie. No surprise. She probably suspected that Mas would throw some kind of wrench into the introduction of the Masao, and she didn't want to be there to witness it.

No Oily. Wasn't he one of the big shots at Everbears? The Shigeo was supposed to save their hide. Oily would never miss an opportunity to share in the spotlight. Mas's head was starting to pound again. And no Jimi Jabami—wait a minute, was that him on the other side of the room? Why was he in a suit? Mas found himself getting dizzy, losing his balance.

"Whoa, are you all right?" Rosa was at his side, steadying him. She was wearing the same black shirt and cargo pants that she'd worn yesterday. Her hair had a halo of frizz. She obviously hadn't showered or groomed herself for at least a day. Mas was surprised to see her at the press conference in plain sight of Linus.

After Mas regained his footing, Rosa pointed to the TV cameras in the back row. "This is your doing, isn't it?"

Actually, it was Genessee's. She'd been the one to contact the media, although only after Mas asked her to do it. There was no other way. He couldn't bear to think of the crates and crates of Masaos that would be grown and harvested throughout the coast, and who knows, even around the nation and the world.

"My group's members had texted me that something big was going to go down here. I had to see it for myself."

Like lookie-loos who wanted to see car crashes and a man with two heads, thought Mas.

"Look, I'm here to back you up. Support you. We all will."

Mas was surprisingly moved. He really didn't care for big-mouth protesters or rich hippies, but at this point, he would take what he could get.

Rosa left to join her protesting friends. Her presence

had actually settled him down a bit. He balled his fists and stretched out his fingers. Looking down at the linoleum floor, he noticed a pair of sturdy black shoes on the man standing next to him.

"Quite a crowd here," Sergeant Salgado said. "You wouldn't expect it for a couple of new strawberries."

Mas grunted and tried to move down a few feet, but a still photographer sitting cross-legged on the floor was blocking his way.

"A judge is going to sign off on that order to exhume Shug's casket. It will probably be coming out tomorrow. If you want to share some information, this would be the time to do it."

Mas's mouth felt raw. "Excuse," Mas said, and Salgado easily let him go. He went to the bathroom to splash cold water onto his face. After patting down his closed eyelids and cheeks, he opened his eyes, only to stare at the mirrored image of his enemy, Linus Verdorben.

"Magnificent work, really magnificent, Mas." After wiping his hand with a paper towel, Linus pounded Mas's back as if they were on the same sports team. He was wearing slacks, a bow tie, and high-toned suspenders.

"Getting all these media people—fantastic. You exceeded my expectations. I mean, with that stunt with the Impala and my fence, I got a better sense of what you were made of."

Still facing the mirror, Linus parted his lips to check if any food particles were stuck in his teeth. "I see you're dressed for the occasion, but it's really not necessary. I'll do all the talking."

The fluorescent lights above the mirror were beginning

to hurt Mas's eyes. Linus was obviously changing his game plan. Instead of covering up the secret ingredient of the Masao, he'd decided to make it front-page news.

"Nobody will eatsu your berry."

"Yes, you're right. That's probably true. It may, however, be a hot commodity among some fetish groups. But we'll be famous, you and I, Mas. We'll be a sensation all over the world. You see, I figure that beating strawberry yellows, that's a limited audience. Just breeder, farmers, and the ag world would be interested in that. But this—I'll be listed in every genetics paper. I'll be on Wikipedia. And you will be, too."

Linus smiled as if he had just won the Lotto.

Mas, on the other hand, felt like he'd been slammed with a ton of bricks. He fled the bathroom and tried to escape the building, but the sheriff's deputies had moved in, blocking his exit.

Then came the audio feedback.

"Shh, shh." The cameramen put on their headphones and adjusted their microphones. "The press conference is starting."

CHAPTER SEVENTEEN

Today is an exciting day in strawberry history, and I'm glad you can all be here to witness the introduction of two strawberry varieties, varieties that will be our response to strawberry yellows." The head of the commission was standing at the podium. He was half Jimi's age and didn't know squat about strawberries. Yet that didn't stop him from droning on and on about the business. "Our industry is more than a century old, and we have been at a crossroads. Today will determine the course of our future."

Jimi's throat felt dry. He'd been fighting a cold these past few days. He hoped his voice would last throughout the day, enough for him to thank all those who would be congratulating him.

Billy was asked to speak on behalf of Everbears. He came prepared with a computer slide show that was full of strawberry family-tree charts. Jimi actually found it somewhat interesting, but the rest of the crowd apparently did not. The man next to Jimi began tapping his foot on the bottom rung of the folding chair in front of him. One woman even audibly sighed. Another man kept shifting his weight, causing his chair to creak.

It probably didn't help that Billy was a rotten public speaker. Shug, on the other hand, was a snake-oil salesman able to promise the moon to anyone who was gullible enough to listen. He had no shame, that was for sure. At least his son seemed to have a little more sense.

"We are calling this new berry the 'Shigeo.' As some of you know, that was my father's full name." Billy's monotone voice then skipped, as if it was a scratched record on a turntable. And then it skipped again.

Was this grown man going to cry? Jimi couldn't believe it. He felt like spitting, but he swallowed his disgust instead. In a few minutes, everyone would be on their feet, clapping for Jimi Jabami and his new career and incarnation, the Maker of the Strawberry in the Twenty-first Century.

Billy coughed away his emotion.

Clay Gorman stood up. In his trademark long-sleeved gray t-shirt, he looked ever the pipsqueak that he was. And while Billy was certainly no orator, Clay was even worse. Billy was John F. Kennedy next to his boss.

"The Shigeo is really a great berry. We hope you enjoy it and we brought some for you to try."

Men and women in polo shirts began passing out clamshell containers of strawberries while Clay posed for photos with Billy. Jimi practically barked at the young man offering him some berries, almost causing an accident. *No Shigeos for me. Good riddance.*

The head of the commission was back at the dais. He pulled the microphone back up and introduced Sugarberry. "As most of you know, we lost one of our breeding pioneers this month, Shug Arai. He had devoted his life to the development of the best berry, and unbeknown to many of us, had been working on a lifelong project up to the day he died. His associate, Dr. Linus Verborden, will be providing details on this special berry. Dr. Verborden. . . ."

Linus, fingering his suspenders, rose from his seat. Jimi, meanwhile, smoothed down his hair.

"Stop!" a familiar voice called out from the depths of the crowd. The legs of folding chairs squeaked against the floor as people got up and moved to create a pathway for a couple walking toward the front. Minnie and Oily. Someone followed them, a slight figure with a mini Afro.

Whatthe—

Minnie went straight for the microphone. "I am the widow of Shug Arai, and I want to make an important announcement. I am a co-owner of this patent now, and I refuse to let it be licensed to anyone."

Jimi was confused. Why were the Arais against the Masao now? He scanned the crowd and saw the miserable little gardener, Mas, in the back by the cameramen. His hands on his knees, he looked stunned as well.

The reporters sitting in the front row straightened their backs and leaned forward.

"The Masao, I believe, would prove injurious to the cooperative, and I won't let it be released."

The reporters began to pepper Minnie with questions.

"What do you mean, 'injurious'?" one called out.

"Would it be a financial liability?"

'What's wrong with the Masao?"

Linus attempted to talk over the reporters. "You are technically not the co-owner, Minnie. Sugarberry is. And as the co-inventor of the Masao, I'm here to tell you that it is a revolutionary berry."

Yes, Jimi said silently, *because its lineage goes back to the Taro.*

"We are part of the cooperative," Minnie shot back, "and we object to the introduction of the Masao."

All attention was on Minnie.

"You all have known me and Shug for years, some even decades. Trust me when I say that the release of this berry will endanger the future of our cooperative, not to mention our industry."

"What's wrong with it?" the question arose again.

"I can't say. I'm sorry, but I can't. If I did, our reputation would be damaged immediately. I cannot let that happen and I won't let that happen."

Circles of strawberry growers grew closer together, intensifying with energy. Mini-tornadoes of reactions whipped through the Sugarberry group, dressed in white shirts, and the Everbears members, dressed in red. The room filled with noise.

Jimi tried to make eye contact with Linus, but the breeder himself seemed overwhelmed. His arms were outstretched, his palms facing the ground, as if he was attempting to steady himself in a moving boat.

A *hakujin* man rose. It was Sperber, a member of Sugarberry. "I object, too."

A Filipino man got up. Pabalan. "I object."

Another Japanese grower, Ichida. "I object."

A *hakujin* woman. Eisert. "I object."

The objections continued. Pretty soon at least a dozen growers were standing. All part of the Sugarberry cooperative.

A few of them cast glances toward Jimi, halfway expecting him to join them. But he remained silent. All he cared about was the announcement, "Jimi Jabami, Sugarberry's new breeder."

Mas could not believe what he was seeing. Minnie and Oily were trying to prevent the release of the Masao. And how did Genessee get up here? Genessee, wearing a colorful print dress, turned around and searched the crowd. Finally her eyes found Mas's. She smiled, a slice of dazzling white.

"Dr. Verdorben, can you tell us why you think your new berry is revolutionary?" a reporter asked.

A ring tone from Minnie's cell phone rang out.

"Of course." Linus gathered himself together, smoothing down his shirt. He was approaching the podium when Minnie, getting off the phone, took control of the microphone again.

"There is no Masao. The Masaos have been destroyed," Minnie reported. She shook her phone in the air to express her glee.

Linus glared and pulled the microphone from Minnie. "Yes, there was a mishap in my test fields in Castroville. But I still have the mothers in storage up in Northern California."

Another tussle for the microphone.

"No, sir, you do not. I just got confirmation that the Masaos were destroyed as of 11:17 a.m. today."

"What's going on?" one of the cameramen said, removing his earphones.

Mas tried to let the news settle in his head. *The Masaos had been destroyed.* Mas knew that strawberry farmers needed to store the runners, or additional growth of the mothers, in a cold area. Back in the late 1940s, Sugarberry was using a storage facility near the Sierra Nevadas that was owned by a Nisei who'd been in the same Poston block as the Arais. Minnie must have ordered the execution of the Masaos, and the word was in—the deed was done.

Linus's face darkened. "You had no right," he said to Minnie.

"According to our living trust, it's legally my storage facility now."

Dazed, Linus reached for the edge of the podium so he wouldn't lose his balance.

The strawberry commission spokesman spoke into the microphone. "Well, this concludes our press conference for today."

The reality of what just transpired was starting to sink into Mas's chest. *Was it over? Was it really over?*

Jimi bumped into other growers as he rushed the stage. *What just happened?* Here he'd spent so much time trying to squash the Masao, and now technically it was dead. But what about him? What about his new position?

"The announcement," Jimi said to Linus, "what about the announcement about me becoming a Sugarberry breeder?"

Linus stumbled from the platform, almost falling to his knees. "The Masao is dead. Dead. How can that be?"

The cameramen began to disassemble their equipment.

"Why the hell did we come here?"

"I have to get over to Silicon Valley now."

"I know a great taco place around the corner."

"Great, I'll follow you."

Mas felt someone tugging on his suit jacket.

"What's going on, Mas?" Now a completely different style and color, Evelyn's hair looked like strips of fried bacon. "Someone at my hairdresser's said something was happening here."

Mas ignored Evelyn, going in the opposite direction of the crowd.

"Genessee," he called out.

Finally, she was in front of him. Her cotton dress made out of an Indian print accentuated her tiny waist. "I spoke to Minnie this morning, and she thought I should get up here. I was on the next plane for San Jose. Oily was able to connect her with a patent attorney, and we figured it was worth a try. I'm so happy for you, Mas."

A ring of white-shirted Sugarberry members had surrounded Minnie, while Oily attempted to insert himself in some last-minute photographs with Clay and Billy, who proudly held a bowlful of Shigeos.

Evelyn, meanwhile, had caught up to Mas. "Hi, you must be Genessee," She extended her hand. "I'm an old friend of Mas's. We are all part of the same gang."

Genessee, returning Evelyn's smile, accepted the handshake.

Mas felt his face grow hot. What was Evelyn going to do, say?

"Mas has spoken very highly about you," Evelyn said. "You must be a special lady."

The world had turned upside down in an instant. No more Masaos. No public humiliation. And now here was Evelyn, being buddy-buddy with Genessee.

Minnie had somehow extracted herself from her Sugarberry coop partners to join them. "Jimi Jabami was here," she told Mas. "Where did he go?"

Mas's eyes scanned the room. Jimi was nowhere to be found.

He dismissed the caretaker and went to check in Ats's room. She had been apparently very quiet that morning.

"Ats," he murmured, collapsing in the recliner opposite her bed.

Her eyes were closed. The shape of her face had changed, Jimi noticed. Her cheeks had lost all their fullness, and even the sagging skin underneath her jowls had disappeared. She resembled the queen of spades, just eyes, nose, and barely a mouth visible.

How he wished he could speak to her. And she to him. Perhaps she would have tried to stopped his scheme to poison Shug. She would have told him that bygones were bygones. That the Arais were forced into camps just like the Jabamis were. In terms of the loss of the house and farm, it was *shikataganai*. It could not be helped. She might have blamed herself, her illness. But not enough to give up. She didn't know how to give up. That's one reason he loved her so much.

Without her counsel, he tried not to give up, either. Getting away with Shug's murder was a sign. A sign that he could do more in this world.

Ats stirred, and her eyes seemed to be fluttering open.

"Ats," he said, "the Arais did it to us again. But I'm going to have a strawberry of my own. I'm going to be a breeder, thanks to Linus Verdorben."

Ats's eyes were pools of black, reminding Jimi of her cat's when it went blind.

Both her hands were underneath her comforter. She

slowly pulled out her left hand and extended it toward her husband.

Yes, yes, my sweetheart. My wife.

Jimi got up and clasped the hand that was being offered. All delicate bones barely held together by almost transparent skin.

The comforter moved again. *What was that?* On the right side, something black and metallic.

A blast and Jimi felt a force go through his chest, his rib cage, his heart. The pain stunned him but soon, thankfully, he couldn't feel a thing.

His body slipped to the ground. His hands padded the front of his shirt. It was slippery, like the first rain falling on a dirt road. His eyes were closing, and before they were completely shut, he heard another blast in the room.

CHAPTER EIGHTEEN

Of all the people who would hear the news of the Jabamis' murder-suicide, Oily was the last person Mas would bet would take it so badly. But he did.

He jumped from his seat and stomped out of the room.

Brushing down his upper lip, the assistant district attorney remained in his chair in the middle of Minnie's living room after delivering the news. Not only were Oily, Mas, and Minnie there, but also Evelyn and Genessee. It was the old gang minus Shug but plus one, a very important female one.

"You better talk to him," Minnie told Mas.

Genessee, sitting next to Minnie, nodded her head.

Why does it have to be me?

Oily was a businessman and a playboy, which meant he was an eternal opportunist. When sales were down one day, he always trusted that sales would go up the next. When one marriage failed, he looked forward to the next one. The fact that Ats had given up on Jimi, not to mention on herself, distressed Oily to no end.

"Ats was the one who always pulled us together," Oily said as they stood in the kitchen.

Mas had been away from their circle for so long that he didn't quite understand what Oily was talking about.

"Every birthday she'd remember. Every time someone was sick, she'd be there with chicken soup. She took care of us. She'd never give up on life."

Mas thought Oily was being a little *ogesa*, exaggerating Ats's role, because if she were so important to them, where were they when she needed them most?

"Maybe dis way she tryin' to keep Jimi from doing bad things," Mas said. From what more he didn't know.

When the two of them finally went to rejoin the group, the attorney was on his way out. "Let me know what you're planning to do," he told Minnie. "You'll have to get your own lawyer to stop it."

Hearing the word "lawyer" from a lawyer made Mas feel queasy. After the door closed behind him, Mas asked, "Whatsu goin' on?"

Seated in her place on the couch, Minnie squeezed one of its cushions. "A judge has cleared the Smiths' request to exhume Shug's casket."

Mas stood back and watched his friends wrestle with this new development.

"That's sacrilegious. You can tell the judge that it's against your religion," Evelyn said.

"But most Buddhists cremate, and I buried Shug, just in case the toxicology report came up fishy. So there goes that argument."

"I'll find you a lawyer, Minnie," Oily said. "We have a good one at Everbears."

"I don't know if a corporate lawyer would have the expertise to handle something like this," Genessee said.

Nobody said anything for a moment. Outside, a garbage

truck making its weekly rounds beeped its warning signal.

"What do you think, Mas?" Minnie asked. Both she and Genessee looked up at him, expectedly.

Mas thought about Shug, the kind of man that he was, at least before the Masao. That man believed in justice, that if you did something wrong, you needed to pay for it. Maybe letting Mas take the fall for the theft of the lizard statue had been a thorn in his side. Since he mentioned it to Oily so many years afterwards, Shug apparently still felt guilty even for a little thing like that. He would want whoever killed Laila, no matter how dear, to face the consequences. Mas's chest heaved as he took in a big breath. "I thinksu Shug would want to be dug up."

Mas felt bad leaving Genessee in the hands of his friends, especially Evelyn. He did, however, have some business to tend to.

Chiquita bonita, the gardener who was at the mortuary on the day of the funeral had said. Pretty girl. And then he added, *Chinita*. Chinese. Mas knew that for the gardener *Chinita* was the end-all word for anyone Asian. And he knew that one person in their circle that would fit that description.

On this drive, Mas took the long way. He completely avoided Hecker Pass; even though Jimi was gone and he was in a new car, Mas didn't want to tempt fate.

She didn't seem surprised to see Mas in the doorway of her dorm room. In fact, sitting at her desk next to her long twin bed, she looked relieved.

The circles under her eyes had gotten darker.

"Where are they?" she asked.

"Who?"

"The police."

"They'su not here."

Alyssa got up in her bare feet to look down the hallway. Completely empty. She pulled out a chair at another desk. "You can sit down."

Mas was surprised by this newfound hospitality. He wasn't going to turn it down and entered the small room. Most of the facing wall was full of windows, so the afternoon sun poured in, causing him to squint as he faced Alyssa, who was back at her desk. Neither of them said anything for a while. Alyssa played with one of her pencils, twirling it around in circles on a blank yellow pad.

"How come I've never seen you before Grandpa's funeral?"

"Haven't been here long time."

"You like L.A.?"

"Itsu *orai*."

"I have some cousins there. In Orange County. On my mother's side."

"Orange County, nice place," Mas lied.

Alyssa twisted her hair up in a bun, securing it in place with her pencil. "I wasn't that close to Grandpa," she finally admitted.

"Oh, yah?"

"I think he liked boys better. He spent more time with Zac, I think."

"You'zu close to your auntie."

Alyssa put her hands in her lap and swallowed. "I used to be close to my dad."

The sound of the hallway door opening and closing. Feet padding the floor. They both waited as a nearby door was unlocked and then shut.

Alyssa was apparently done with small talk. She went right to the core of her anguish. "I didn't mean to kill her. I know how lame that sounds. Like every TV show, right? But I didn't mean to. It happened so fast. One second we were arguing there in the greenhouse. She was being so mean to me. Saying I was a no-good daughter, that I was making my dad feel bad by not talking to him. How does she get off telling me that I'm not a good daughter?

"So I called her some names. Really bad names. And then she starts insulting Grandpa. The night before his funeral. She says that I'm just a kid; that Grandpa was involved with weird stuff and everyone's going to find out about it soon. I couldn't stand it anymore. So I just reached over for that bat. Zac and I used to play with that bat all the time. It was like the bat was placed there, right next to me. I just wanted her to shut up. So I took it and swung. And it was finally quiet."

Alyssa pulled her left leg up onto her chair. "I was going to tell Aunt Robin right away. Brandon and I were staying over at her place. I wanted to. But she was out like I was, trying to find Dad. That's how this all started, you know. Laila came to Robin's house, all crying, a total mess. She and Dad had been in a fight, and he took off. Drinking and driving. So Robin goes in her car to look for him. I don't want to be alone with her. Laila. Actually she's the last person I want to be with. But Robin asks me to. She can't do her job if Laila's with her. Laila's so antsy; I can't stay in that house with her, so we decide to drive around, too.

"Going to the Stem House was my idea. I knew Dad goes over there when he gets stressed out. I wasn't planning to hurt her. It just happened."

"What about your brotha?"

"Zac? Oh, he slept through the whole thing." Alyssa rolled her eyes. "But Robin knows. I told her after the funeral. I was going to tell her in the morning, but she got that call to go to the Stem House. I was freaking out. I took the bat with me early, before the funeral. I didn't know what to do with it. I cleaned it real good in Auntie's laundry room. I was planning to maybe burn it or drive it to the dump, but there wasn't enough time."

Alyssa put the side of her index finger next to her lip. "I figure Grandpa's casket was the best place. We were supposed to leave things there for him, anyway. I thought he was going to get cremated, but I guess Grandma had changed her mind."

"They'su gonna open up the coffin soon."

"Yeah, yeah, I heard."

Mas was surprised that the news had reached her already.

"My fingerprints are all over that bat."

Clouds moved in front of the sun, causing the light in the room to soften.

"My aunt's on her way to pick me up. I'm going to tell the police what I did to Laila." The girl covered her face with her hands. Each fingernail was painted a different color. "I'm so, so scared," she said. "What are they going to do with me?"

Mas felt awful, just sitting there while the girl cried. He remembered one day Shug asking him out of the blue: "Mas, just how bad was it?" They were helping a Salinas farmer haul some tomatoes; dried seeds shaped like green teardrops were all over their clothes.

"Huh?" Mas didn't know what Shug was talking about.

"Hiroshima. The A-bomb." Shug removed a rolled-up magazine from his back pocket. It was old, a 1946 issue from three years ago. A publication called *The New Yorker* that had devoted its whole issue to Hiroshima.

His hand on his hip, Mas watched as a couple of produce men examined the crates of tomatoes. He was surprised that Shug was bringing this up for the first time after living under the same roof for a year. But something seemed to be on his second cousin's mind those days. He tended to go off on his own for long walks or drives. Mas didn't know what to tell him. "A lot of friends dead."

"You don't seem worse for wear. Never hear you *monku*."

"You no *monku*, too."

Shug let out a laugh, which actually sounded more like a hacking cough. "Maybe that's the Japanese way. But Mas, sometimes when I think about my dad and mom and all they lost during the war, this anger comes out, out of nowhere. And sometimes, I hate to say it, I get mad at them."

"Whatchu mad at?"

"Not sure, really. Not that they could have done anything. I don't know. It's just that I don't know what to do with the anger."

Mas had no advice to give. He felt like he was always running from one place to another. Working in the hot sun and sweating. That seemed to help, too. But that didn't seem to be the solution.

Mas, now looking at Alyssa, didn't know what to say. He wouldn't lie and say that everything was going to be all right. Because there wasn't any guarantee about that. But she was young, just like Mas and Shug had been. There was time. Time was on her side.

Genessee was staying at Minnie's house, but Mas tried to keep out of there as much as he could. Through everything, Minnie was still unflappable, offering fresh coffee to guests while her world continued to fall apart. Funny thing was, the girl's mother, Colleen, had come out of her rabbit hole as soon as she heard that Alyssa needed her. Her stripe of gray hair had gotten wider, but she seemed more vibrant. It was as if her daughter's predicament had energized her with new purpose.

Billy, on the other hand, seemed to withdraw some, disappearing at odd times in his truck. Mas suspected that guilt was eating away at him—that if he hadn't had a relationship with Laila, maybe his daughter would be with them instead of sitting in a holding cell.

It was past nine in the evening when Mas parked the Impala across from the Stem House. Someone was there already. Billy in his pickup truck.

They both got out of their vehicles and laughed for a moment underneath a light by a telephone pole. It was funny that the Stem House, no matter its current state, was their elixir during dark times.

"Came from the jail," Billy said, "to see Alyssa. Her arraignment is tomorrow. The attorney thinks we can get her out on bail."

Mas didn't know what to say.

"We had a good talk. We hadn't spoken to each other like that in, I don't know, years." Billy bent over and Mas could see silvery tears hang onto his eyelashes, like dew on blades of grass.

Billy didn't even bother to wipe his eyes. "I made a mess of everything, Mas. I don't know if I can make it right."

They remained silent for a few moments and then Billy walked toward the small plot of land by the greenhouses. Mas followed.

"You know, after Dad died, I thought about going back to Sugarberry. But Mom told me not to. She said I had to find my own way in this industry. As long as I worked for Sugarberry, I'd be seen as Shug's son."

They stopped before a barren patch of dirt where an earlier generation of the Masaos had been growing. For a moment, Mas thought about asking him about Clay Gorman and his relationship with Laila. But then he reconsidered. *Why? Why put a wedge between Billy and his Everbears boss?* Laila was gone, so what was the use?

Billy knelt and patted the ground. "After the press conference, Linus was fired. Sugarberry's going to be hiring a new hybridizer. A young guy, he's in his thirties and has been working in Florida. He's actually the son of a woman who works in the packing shed. You might have been packing clamshells with her."

Mas pictured the brown faces of his co-workers.

Everything came full circle.

"We're going to cremate Dad now. They have the bat as evidence and now we can do it right. It's the way Dad would have wanted."

A seagull, most likely lost, flew above the Stem House.

"I never really talked much to him. Mostly on our fishing trips. One time he told me that we needed to be one step better than everyone else. Because our last name was Arai. Because we were Japanese. I think by making the Masao, he truly thought he would be helping people. Pushing something to the next level."

Billy looked up at Mas. "What I'm trying to say is I don't think my father was using you. I think he honestly felt that he was creating something to honor you."

Mas wondered if that was true. He wasn't sure, but decided to believe it. That was the best thing that a friend could do.

"Well," Billy rose, brushing dirt from his hands to his jeans. "I have to go. I have a long day tomorrow."

"Me and Genessee leavin' in the morning."

"You'll probably be glad to be getting out of here. I'm sure you feel that you've been cursed here. Anyway, I'll be at Mom's first thing to see you off."

Billy got into his pickup and pulled out into the dirt road.

Mas stood alone while darkness fell over the hushed fields. The outline of the Stem House strangely comforted him, as if it were the center of a compass. Everything that had traveled away from it would still be connected to its magnetic force.

In spite of everything that happened, Watsonville was not a curse. It could never be one. When Shug's mother, Satoko, passed away, Mas came to her funeral with Chizuko and Mari. In the Impala, in fact. Chizuko had packed an old Broadway department-store box with lines of *onigiri* with pickled plums in their centers. As Mas drove along the 101 highway, Chizuko carefully handed him a rice ball in a moistened paper towel, which blew out the window, leaving him with sticky fingers around the steering wheel.

From the seaside they traveled through the green hills to the flatness of farmland. The two-lane highway cut into acres of ranches, lines of green crops stretching out forever.

Normally Chizuko was the master of facts and knowledge, but not in the country. Here it was Mas who knew all.

"Dad, what's this?" asked Mari.

"Spinach."

"What's that?"

"Cauliflower."

"What's this?"

"Broccoli."

Mari would press her small nose against the window as the green rows blurred into one another.

The crops bore no obvious signs of identification, but Mas knew what to look for. The shape, color, and size of leaves. The direction the plant was growing. The time of the year.

This had been his world for two years—his education, in fact. An education that had been better than any junior college degree.

He'd learned much from Shug's father, Wataru Arai. For

all the time Mas had known him, Wataru was pretty much bald, except for a little fuzz on top of his head that resembled algae on a rock in a tidepool.

After dinner on warm summer days, they'd sit on the steps of the Stem House, speaking in Japanese.

"This is my house," Wataru said proudly. "But it all can disappear. In a fire. Or in a war."

He stretched out his legs and rubbed his knees. "If it's taken away, I'm *orai. Honto*, really. Because my children are all grown. Making their own mistakes. Making their own lives."

Mas knew that Wataru liked to talk with him because he was among the few young men who actually could speak and understand Japanese. "Nothing's better than this country. A Number Two, Number Three son can make his life here, a new life. That's why when they open up for Issei like me to get naturalized, I will."

It was 1950, and for a Japanese immigrant to talk about becoming a citizen meant he had an active imagination.

Mas didn't want to be a wet blanket. "Maybe, *Ojisan*," he said. "Maybe someday."

As it turned out, Wataru had been a bit of a prophet, because what he predicted came true. In 1952, Issei could become naturalized. But he, unfortunately, had died a few months earlier.

What would *Ojisan* have thought of all of this? Mas wondered. Would he have been ashamed of what Shug had tried to do, of how Billy lost the Stem House, of his grand-daughter killing Laila? Would he yell out in pain or hide his face from his neighbors?

No, *Ojisan* was not that kind of man. Mas imagined

Wataru Arai standing straight, lifting his head high. For him, Watsonville was a place of second chances, or maybe third or fourth chances.

"Ready?" Mas asked.

"Ready," Genessee replied.

Mas felt a bit odd carrying Genessee's bags to the Impala, as if they were off on a honeymoon trip. They weren't going on a trip, after all. They were going home.

He closed the trunk and looked at the line of people assembled in the driveway. Minnie, Oily, Evelyn, Billy. Even Victor had brought Miguel out in a wheelchair. At his age and some of their ages, Mas wasn't sure if he would see some of them again alive. He held each face in his embattled brain, hoping that he wouldn't forget any of them.

Genessee opened the passenger door and got in. Mas lingered for a moment, inhaling the wet, soil-tinged air one last time. Sitting in the driver's seat, he started the engine, wiping the window with the edge of his sweatshirt. Through the smeared glass, he saw a flurry of hands waving, lips mouthing soundless goodbyes, sending them off down the street and beyond.

ABOUT THE AUTHOR

NAOMI HIRAHARA is the Edgar-winning author of the Mas Arai mystery series, including *Gasa Gasa Girl, Summer of the Big Bachi, Snakeskin Shamisen,* and *Blood Hina,* as well as the children's novel *1001 Cranes.* She lives in Southern California.